His to Claim

ALSO BY OPAL CAREW

Bliss

Forbidden Heat

Secret Ties

Six

Blush

Swing

Twin Fantasies

Pleasure Bound

Total Abandon

Secret Weapon

Insatiable

Illicit

His to Command

His to Possess

His to Claim

Opal Carew

St. Martin's Griffin
New York

HIS TO CLAIM. Copyright © 2014 by Opal Carew. All rights reserved. Printed in the United States of America. For information, address St. Martin's Press, 175 Fifth Avenue, New York, N.Y. 10010.

The following chapters in this book were previously published as individual e-books.
His to Claim #1: No Strings. Copyright © 2014 by Opal Carew.
His to Claim #2: Savage Kiss. Copyright © 2014 by Opal Carew.
His to Claim #3: Rock Hard. Copyright © 2014 by Opal Carew.
His to Claim #4: Wild Ones. Copyright © 2014 by Opal Carew.
His to Claim #5: Breaking Storm. Copyright © 2014 by Opal Carew.
His to Claim #6: Perfect Rhythm. Copyright © 2014 by Opal Carew.

www.stmartins.com

The Library of Congress Cataloging-in-Publication Data is available upon request.

ISBN 978-1-250-05282-7 (trade paperback)
ISBN 978-1-4668-5468-0 (e-book)

St. Martin's Griffin books may be purchased for educational, business, or promotional use. For information on bulk purchases, please contact Macmillan Corporate and Premium Sales Department at 1-800-221-7945, extension 5442, or write specialmarkets@macmillan.com.

First Edition: September 2014

10 9 8 7 6 5 4 3 2 1

To Matt.
I miss you,
but I'm glad
you're following
your dream.

Acknowledgments

As always, thank you to my wonderful editor, Rose Hilliard, and my fabulous agent, Emily Sylvan Kim. Thanks to my husband, Mark, who is my biggest fan (as I am his.) Thank you to Laurie, who helps me with so many things. Thank you to my two sons, Matt and Jason, for always being supportive of my work. A special thank-you to Matt, for helping me research setting for this and the previous connected book, and for helping me figure out a band tour that makes sense. Finally, thank you to the lovely Katy Cartwright for the artistic inspiration, information about an artist's journey, and for designing the lovely bluebird tattoo for me!

His to Claim

No Strings

Melanie's heart stopped as the bell over the door rang and she glanced up to see a tall man in a dark gray suit walk in. Something about his tall, broad-shouldered form and expensive suit reminded her of Rafe for a moment. But it was just one of her regulars.

"Hey, beautiful. The usual."

They chatted while she fixed him his typical latte, then she handed it to him with a smile. He winked and then headed for the door. She knew he was flirting with her. It had been going on all week, and although he was a very attractive man, she wasn't interested.

She glanced around the store. The few customers were happily chatting over their coffees and there was no sign of a new customer coming into the shop.

"I'm going in the back to grab some more sugar," she said to her friend Sue, the other barista on duty, who was currently refilling the thermoses of milk after their recent rush.

The fast-paced influx of customers had left Melanie a little drained. She wasn't used to being on her feet for eight hours a day. But it was better than the intense attraction to her former boss, Rafe, driving her mad every day.

"Okay. Then, if you don't mind, I'll take my break," Sue said.

Melanie opened the storage cupboard and grabbed a pack of raw sugar, another of white sugar, and some artificial sweetener, then carried them to the lobby and started filling the condiment stand with the small packets. Once done, she returned to the bar and tucked the leftover sugar packets under the counter.

The bell over the door rang, signaling a new customer. Melanie stood up and glanced toward the door to see a man in a charcoal suit talking to Sue. She sighed. It looked like her admirer was back, and she knew Sue would do what she could to play matchmaker. Sue pointed in Melanie's direction and the man turned.

Melanie's heart stopped when she saw his face. This was not the customer who'd been flirting with her all week.

As soon as he saw her, his lips turned up in a sexy, crooked smile—the one that always melted her heart—and he walked toward the bar.

He was a striking figure in his expensive, well-tailored suit that accentuated his tall physique and broad shoulders. His dark, glossy hair was combed back and his stunning sky blue eyes ringed in navy were locked on her.

"Hello, Melanie."

"Mr. Ranier."

He chuckled. "Haven't I always told you to call me Rafe?"

She nodded. His authoritative brother, Dane, had insisted on being called Mr. Ranier, but Rafe had always preferred a more casual address.

"Rafe, what are you doing here?"

"Getting a coffee, for starters." He glanced up at the board. "What do you suggest?"

"Iced coffees are quite popular right now. We have one with a hint of cinnamon and orange." She knew his brother would want a regular coffee, but Rafe was always willing to try something new.

"Sounds good."

"To take with you?" she asked as she reached for a takeout cup.

"Actually, that depends. Can you join me?"

"Of course she can." Sue smiled as she returned to the bar. "In fact, Melanie was just about to go on break."

Melanie glanced at Sue. "I thought you were going now."

"I'll go later." She glanced at Rafe and smiled. "In fact, you go sit and I'll make you both something."

"But if the manager sees . . ." Melanie said under her breath.

"She's gone for the day, and I'm not going to tell."

Melanie walked to a table in the back corner, wanting to be discreet.

"This is cozy," Rafe said as he sat down across from her.

"So why are you here?" Melanie asked with a smile. "Besides the coffee."

"Does there have to be a reason?"

"This isn't anywhere near where you work or where you live."

"Why don't you think I was at a meeting nearby?"

Her eyebrows arched. "Were you?"

He shook his head. "No, I came here to see you."

Her stomach clenched at the admission. She didn't work for him anymore. They had been friendly in the office, but they hadn't been friends. He'd been her boss. There was only one reason she could think of for why he'd be here. The one reason she'd been dreading, and hoping she wouldn't have to deal with.

He wanted to know why she'd quit.

Even though Jessica had ultimately chosen Rafe's brother, Melanie had finally come to terms with the fact that she would never have a chance with Rafe. And she didn't want to tell him.

She'd worked for him for over two years and . . . she'd fallen in love with him. But in all that time, he'd never given her a second look. Then when he'd fallen in love with her best friend, Jessica, it had broken Melanie's heart. It had just been too painful to keep working with him, and to watch the two of them together.

That's why she'd quit.

And she couldn't tell him any of that.

Sue came to the table with two iced coffees, then returned to the bar.

"I was surprised to find you were working as a barista.

It's quite a change from an office environment." He sipped his coffee.

"How did you find out where I was?"

He shrugged. "I checked your personnel file. Someone from this location called for a reference."

"So you just came by to see if I was here?"

"That's right."

She shook her head. "I still don't understand why."

He leaned forward, his sky blue eyes intent. "I just want to make sure you're okay."

She straightened her back. "Of course. Why wouldn't I be?"

"You up and left a good job . . . a job you seemed to be happy at . . . for no good reason. And here you are working at a job for probably minimum wage. I don't get it."

"I needed a change. I like the freedom I have here." And it was true. She might have left to free herself from her obsessive love for Rafe but she'd come to realize that she was seeking an even bigger freedom from the rules she always bound herself by.

"Freedom?"

"I'm not tied to a nine-to-five existence. I'm not tied to a desk. I don't have a boss hovering over me." As soon as she said it, she realized he'd take it the wrong way.

"Did I hover over you? Is that why you left?"

"No, I don't mean that. It was the nature of the job. I couldn't leave my desk without getting someone to cover for me and handle phone calls. I needed to keep on top of both your schedule and your brother's. What I did was totally driven by what other people needed."

"Isn't that true here?"

"People come in for coffee, and maybe something to eat. It's not a big commitment.".

He frowned. "I'm sorry, Melanie. I didn't realize you were unhappy."

"No, it's not that. I wasn't really unhappy."

"If I had known, I could have found something else for you. Something you'd enjoy doing. It's a big company." He leaned toward her. "We still could. Say the word and I'll call personnel."

Sweet, helpful Rafe. "No, thanks. I'm happy here." She finished her iced coffee and stood up. "I should get back to work."

"Wait, Melanie. Just give me another minute."

She sank back into the chair.

"Please tell me one thing."

She stared at him, dreading whatever question he was about to ask.

"Did I do something?"

"No, Rafe. You didn't do a thing."

In fact, that was the whole problem.

As soon as her shift was over, Melanie changed and grabbed the bottle of nail polish she'd stashed in her purse this morning. She couldn't wear polish to work, and she was a real fanatic, so she carried it with her and put it on after her shift if she was going out. She was meeting Jessica after work and she hated going out with naked nails.

She rolled the bottle between her hands to mix it up without creating air bubbles. It was actually part of a collection of polishes Rafe had given her to thank her for helping him pick out a gift for Jessica. He was always so thoughtful.

She brushed on the polish. A simple two-coater in turquoise, but with trendy black speckles for interest. She finished with her favorite fast-dry topcoat.

She didn't see her former roommate, Jessica, much these days. Jessica had moved into Mr. Ranier's place. And who wouldn't? Not only was she staying with the man of her dreams, who happened to be beyond gorgeous, he was also a billionaire who lived at the Ritz-Carlton residence, where his luxury apartment had a spectacular view of the Philadelphia skyline.

Melanie grabbed a bus to the great little deli she and Jessica had discovered a month ago.

When Melanie stepped into the restaurant, she saw Jessica at a table by the window, a drink in front of her.

"Hey, how's it going?" Melanie asked as she tossed her purse on a chair, then sat down across from Jessica. But she didn't need to ask because the glow in Jessica's face said it all. Now there was a woman in love!

"We picked out the flowers today," Jessica said. "It was so funny being in a florist shop with Dane. The two women who worked there stared at him in awe, and they seemed intimidated by him, even though he was as charming as could be."

"Well, he does have a very commanding presence. You know that." She leaned in close. "I'm not surprised he brings that quality into the bedroom," she said with a grin.

"Does he ever." Jessica laughed, not at all embarrassed. That's one of the things Melanie loved about her friend. Jessica was willing to jump into an exciting situation and run with it.

Jessica had also told her about the exciting Dominance/submission relationship she had going with Mr. Ranier, which made Melanie weak in the knees just thinking about.

"You're really lucky, you know that?" She smiled. "You found the right guy and now you're getting married."

Jessica nodded. "I know it. But as you recall, it wasn't easy."

"Nothing ever is."

Jessica reached out and placed her hand over Melanie's. "You know, there's no reason you and Rafe—"

"Jessica, forget it. It'll never happen."

"It could."

"No. It didn't happen after two years of working together. Most of that time was before he met you. But he was attracted to you right off." She shook her head sadly. "I have to face it. The guy just isn't into me."

"It's all in the context. You were his secretary—"

"And you were Mr. Ranier's personal assistant."

Jessica squeezed Melanie's hand. "If you gave Rafe a chance to get to know you outside the office, I'm sure everything would change."

"Look, can we just change the subject?" Melanie had been intending to tell Jessica about Rafe coming into the store today, but not now. Jessica meant well, but Melanie just didn't want to think about what might have been. More like, what couldn't be. "Are you going to tell me what the surprise is you told me about?"

Jessica smiled broadly. "Okay. Well, I know that your

birthday isn't until next week, but I want to give you your gift now."

She handed Melanie a lilac envelope with her name written in Jessica's lovely script on the front. Melanie opened it and inside found a gift certificate for a tattoo studio. She'd once told Jessica that she'd always wanted a tattoo, but they were expensive and she couldn't justify it on her budget.

Melanie stared at the certificate. "This is so generous of you. I really shouldn't accept."

"It's from Dane, too, and he insisted. We all miss you at Ranier Industries, and we hope your tattoo gives you a little reminder every day of how much we care about you."

"Okay, I'm not going to argue. You two are . . ." Her voice quavered a little, so she just nodded while she drew in a deep breath. She shrugged. ". . . terrific."

She'd never had a friend as sweet and considerate as Jessica. The two women had taken to each other instantly—it was like they'd known each other for years. Melanie believed this could be a lifetime friendship.

"So how did you pick the place?" Melanie had been asking around for recommendations. If she was going to have something inked onto her body she wanted to ensure that the place was reputable, high quality, and that the artist was talented.

"I asked a friend who is very discerning. The artist you'll be seeing is Charlie. He came highly recommended and the online samples of his work are gorgeous. He books up pretty fast, so I called last week and made an appointment for you on Saturday, since I know that's your day off, and I also knew you'd be anxious to get it. You can move it if it's not convenient, but it'll probably mean waiting a couple of weeks."

"No way. I want to do this as soon as possible. Of course you'll go with me, right?"

Jessica frowned. "I'm afraid not. I already have plans and I can't change them."

"Oh."

Jessica smiled. "I promise, I'll try to be there for the next, brand new, wild and crazy thing you do."

Melanie nodded. "It's a deal."

As Melanie opened the door to Devil's Ink, she was greeted by the cheerful tinkle of a bell. She stepped into the clean, brightly lit studio. The walls were a warm brick red and covered with framed artwork of large, detailed tattoo designs.

There was a glass reception counter on one side and black chairs along two walls with a coffee table covered with magazines and binders. A large tropical plant stood in one corner.

"Can I help you?" A tall, lanky woman in a navy tank top and jeans, with several face piercings and her arms sleeved with tattoos, stood up from her chair behind the counter.

"I have an appointment with Charlie at three o'clock. I just wanted to be here ahead of time."

"Sure. There's some design books on the table there. Coffee machine's over there. Help yourself."

"Thanks." Melanie sat in one of the waiting chairs and leaned forward to riffle through the black binders laid out on the low, square table in front of her. She grabbed one and opened it, then scanned through it. There were a broad range of designs, sorted into categories. The shading on the designs was very well done, something she'd been told to watch for.

The bell over the door tinkled and in her peripheral vision, she saw a man in well-worn jeans, a chain dangling from his belt loop into his pocket, walk past her.

The man walked to the counter. Melanie glanced over the book at his back and couldn't help but admire his broad shoulders and thick, muscular arms, showcased by the black tank top he wore.

Two men stepped into the room from a hallway, one a tall, bald man with a beard, his solid chest, arms, and neck covered with tattoos, and the other a man with white gauze on his bicep.

"I'll be right with you," the bald man said to the newcomer. "Hey, Rika. Bob's done."

"Be right there, Charlie," the tall, lanky woman called from the other side of a doorway, then she walked back to the counter and smiled at the man with the gauze.

The bald man, who seemed to be the artist Melanie was here to see, turned to his next client and said, "Okay, now let me see what I'm working with."

The new client pulled off his tank top and walked toward him. Melanie's gaze landed on the hard, rippling muscles.

"So, you're sure you don't want me to alter the moth now that the chick has dumped you? Maybe change it to an angel?"

This man had a moth tattoo? Rafe had gotten a moth tattoo when he'd been dating Jessica.

"Naw. An angel's not my style."

The sound of the man's familiar voice stunned Melanie.

The artist chuckled. "Yeah, until a chick asks you for it, right?"

She raised her gaze up the broad, tattoo-covered chest, to the man's face.

"Rafe?"

She put down the book she'd been scanning and stared at him with wide eyes. She never would have believed Rafe would ever look like *this*. Muscle bound, inked, and breath-takingly hunky in a sexy bad-boy way. He was gorgeous beyond belief in his designer suits but, man, that was nothing compared to what lay underneath.

Rafe turned to her. "Melanie?" His lips turned up in that wide smile of his, paired with the warmth in his eyes that always made her feel special. "What are you doing here?"

Rafe gazed at Melanie. Her dark blonde hair hung loose, rather than tied back like she usually wore it at the office and the coffee shop she worked at now. It cascaded past her smooth, bare shoulders in soft waves, gleaming in the sunlight flowing through the big window.

She shrugged. "Same as you. Getting a tattoo."

His lips turned up in a grin. "Really?"

Charlie grabbed a piece of paper Rika handed him, probably the artwork Charlie had worked up from the basic design Rafe had sent him.

Rafe watched as Melanie walked toward him.

"I'm afraid I'm a virgin," she said.

Charlie chuckled.

Suddenly, Rafe saw her differently. Not as his sweet, innocent secretary, who wore demure suits and conservative flats. In those jeans and that lace-edged, black camisole top that showed off her shapely form, she looked anything but virginal.

Her cheeks heated. "As far as tattoos, I mean."

Her gaze gliding over his broad shoulders, then down to his abs heated him like the caress of the noonday sun.

"You're obviously very experienced," she said.

Charlie chuckled again.

Rafe found himself tightening at her words, his mind filled with images of her, wide-eyed and vulnerable, lying in his bed. Fuck, what was wrong with him? This was Melanie.

"It's just that, I'm kind of nervous about this. I've always wanted one, but it's so permanent—and I know it's going to hurt."

He quirked his head. "Would you like me to stay with you?" He grinned. "Maybe hold your hand."

She just nodded, and a need to be there for her, and protect her, washed through him.

"Could I watch while you get yours done?"

"You don't have any problem with that, do you, Charlie?"

Charlie grunted. "The more the merrier."

Charlie turned and headed to the hallway leading to his room. Rafe gestured for Melanie to precede him, and he followed her down the hall, his gaze settling on the delightful sway of her hips.

Once in the room, Charlie glanced at Melanie and pointed at a nearby chair. "You can sit there."

Rafe sat down and Melanie watched as Charlie applied the template, then peeled it off.

"That work for you?" Charlie asked.

Rafe was happy with the placement of the design and nodded.

Melanie admired the design he was getting on his chest. It was the words SAVAGE KISS in the shape of a guitar. "That's the name of your band, isn't it?"

Rafe nodded once. "All my life music has been an outlet for me, a way to let go of my anger after one of my father's beatings, or a way to burn off my frustration when I was pushed into a business I wasn't even sure I wanted to be in. So this tat is not only to remember the year I spent with my band, but a symbol of what a huge part of my life music has always been. It saved me when I had nothing else."

"That's beautiful." Melanie eyed the tattoo machine Charlie picked up and seemed to jump at the buzzing sound when he turned it on.

Rafe had done this enough times that he was used to it, so it didn't faze him when Charlie started the outline, but he knew for Melanie, being her first time, she might have a hard time with it. He hoped his relaxed attitude during the whole process would calm her, but he could see the distress in her eyes as she watched the angry swirls taking the shape of a guitar on his chest.

The tattoo took about an hour, and Melanie watched intently the whole time. Once it was done, he stared in the mirror at Charlie's handiwork. Perfect as usual. Anxiety filled Melanie's eyes as she stared at the redness around the edges. Charlie applied cream to the tattoo and placed the gauze over it, then Rafe stood up.

"I guess it's my turn now," Melanie said reluctantly.

"Who's doing yours?" he asked.

"I am," Charlie said. He walked over to the workstation and returned with a template. "Where's it going?"

"Oh, um . . . right here." She pointed to the top of her right breast.

"Okay. You wanna sit or lie down?"

She glanced at the padded table he had by the wall, then shook her head. "I'll sit."

Melanie sat in the leather chair, biting her lip.

"Don't worry. You'll be fine," Rafe said.

She nodded, but looked even more nervous as Charlie sat down and rolled his stool close to her.

"You gonna take off the top, or just pull down the edge?" Charlie asked.

"Oh," she gazed at Rafe, then glanced at the paper template in Charlie's hand, "will it work to just tuck it down?"

"Yeah, why not?"

Rafe's gaze locked on Melanie's fingers as she slowly tugged down the top edge of the fabric, revealing the swell of her breast.

God damn, she was sexy. But he shouldn't be thinking of her that way.

As she pulled the fabric lower, revealing more sweet, creamy flesh, he realized that she didn't work for him anymore, so he could think about her any way he wanted. As long as he didn't act on it.

Unless she wanted him to.

Would she, he wondered.

Charlie placed the paper on her round flesh, and as he rubbed it to make it smooth against her skin, Rafe wished he could be doing that. He longed to feel that lovely curve.

Charlie peeled away the paper, leaving a beautiful design of a bird taking flight.

"Nice." Rafe smiled.

"Thanks. I did the design myself."

Surprise skittered through him. He knew she liked to express herself with color, like her nail polishes, but he hadn't realized she had an artistic bent.

"It's beautiful. You're very talented."

"Thanks."

Her cheeks flushed pink. He didn't know if it was from the compliment, or the fact that half her breast was exposed.

"My parents weren't very supportive of my dreams either. They worked menial jobs and pushed me to go to college to be the family success story, to make all their sacrifices worthwhile. So I went and got my administrative degree, even though I really wanted to go to art school. But they never would have supported that—so the only way I ever got to express myself these past few years is through my nail art. But I really want to bring it back into my life. I love to imagine things and bring them to life through my artwork."

When Charlie turned on the tattoo machine, Melanie jumped at the sound. Rafe stepped to her side and rested his hand on her forearm.

"I'm gonna start now," Charlie said. "You gotta stay real still. Got that?"

She eyed him, nodding uncertainly.

"It's okay. It ain't gonna hurt too much."

Charlie was a little rough around the edges, but he had his compassionate side.

"Okay." But as he leaned toward her, Melanie's hand slipped around Rafe's forearm, and her fingers tightened.

Rafe covered her hand with his. "Breathe."

She drew in a deep breath as Charlie pressed the device to her skin. At the first contact, her eyes widened, but she didn't move.

"You doing okay?" Rafe asked.

She nodded again, watching Charlie work. Rafe watched in fascination as the artist glided the machine over her creamy breast, the skin reddening around the black line of the design as he moved. Melanie continued to breathe deeply, but soon began to relax a little.

He stroked the back of her hand with his thumb. "Not too bad, right?"

She nodded, as if afraid to utter any words.

When Charlie finished the outline, he drew away, getting ready for the shading. This part hurt more.

She gazed down at the design, which was taking shape

nicely. Right now it was just an outline of the bird, but once Charlie filled it in with color, it would come to life.

"Do you want some water?" Rafe asked.

"Yes, thanks."

She drew her delicate hand from his arm and he immediately missed the contact. He grabbed a bottle from the small fridge Charlie had on the side and twisted off the cap for her.

He handed it to her and she took a deep swallow, just as Charlie returned to her side, a number of pigments doled out on his tray in little pools. He dipped the device into one of the blues, then began filling in the wings of the bird. She tensed again, and this time Rafe reached for her hand. She glanced up at him and smiled timidly, then gazed at Charlie's handiwork, her fingers clinging tightly to Rafe's hand.

"So why did you pick a bird?" Rafe asked, hoping to distract her.

"It's a symbol." She laughed tensely. "I guess that's true for everyone. But for me it represents freedom, and that's something I'm trying to embrace right now. Not getting caught up in other people's expectations, and just being true to myself and my own dreams, even if they're impractical."

She took another swallow from the water bottle. The bird took form as Charlie swirled the tattoo machine along her skin. Melanie seemed to want to concentrate on watching Charlie work, so Rafe just continued to stroke her hand. Although she was handling the pain, after a while it seemed to be getting to her, so he drew her hair back from her face, then curled his fingers behind her neck and kneaded the tense muscles. She gazed up at him in surprise.

"That's nice," she said. "Thanks."

She seemed to relax as she gazed at him rather than at the tattoo. There was something in her bright green eyes that disturbed and yet elated him. A warmth that he realized he'd seen before. Had she always looked at him that way and he'd never noticed?

A tightness coiled in his stomach. Or had he chosen not to notice? Shutting it out because, he realized now, he felt the same warmth for her but he would never act on feelings for an employee. He would never put her in that position.

They'd been close when he'd been her boss. At least, they'd shared a friendly camaraderie.

And he'd told her things he wouldn't tell just anyone, like when he'd fallen in love with Jessica during a year of soul searching, then lost her. When he'd found her working for his brother on his return to Philly, he'd hoped for a reconciliation, but that hadn't worked out.

But here was Melanie, looking absolutely sinful as a sheen of sweat appeared on the swell of her cleavage. She bit her full bottom lip, and his gut told him it was worth exploring where this might lead.

Charlie wiped the design with his cloth, then changed pigment. Melanie tensed when he started up again and Rafe continued stroking her neck, pleased that he could help her through this.

Charlie continued filling in the tattoo. Finally, he sat back and stared critically at the bluebird design for a moment, then nodded and smiled. As well he should. It was stunning. Charlie grabbed a big handheld mirror and offered it to her. She took the mirror and held it so she could see the design front on, rather than staring down at it. Her face lit up with a beautiful, beaming smile.

"Oh, it's beautiful!"

"It really is," Rafe agreed, though he found he couldn't drag his gaze from her stunning features.

High cheekbones and soft-looking, heart-shaped lips. A delicate chin and pert little nose. And big emerald green eyes that seemed to glow.

How had he never realized how beautiful she was before?

Charlie applied cream to the tattoo. The sight of his big fingers rubbing vigorously over the soft flesh of her breast sent a little jealously surging through Rafe. And a shot of adrenaline as his groin tightened at the thought of his own hand stroking her breast like that.

Charlie covered the tattoo with gauze and she stood up. Rafe followed her out the door, then to the reception desk.

Rika smiled. A new gem—deep red, probably a garnet—glinted from her lip. He hadn't noticed it when he came into the shop. It was her fifth, joining the blue, green, amber, and purple ones already there.

"I like the new piercing."

Her smile broadened. "Yeah, thanks. Happy with your new ink?"

"I am. As always." He glanced at Melanie.

She nodded. "It's beautiful. He did a fantastic job."

"Good. That's what we like to hear."

Rafe pulled out his credit card and slid it into the small device on the counter. He finished the transaction, then pulled out some twenties and handed them to Rika. "Please give that to Charlie."

"Sure thing." Rika placed the money in an envelope behind the counter.

Melanie placed her bag on the counter.

Rika smiled at her. "Oh, you're all set. Your gift certificate covered it."

"Okay, but . . . um . . ."

"If you're worried about the tip, hon, it was enough to cover that, too. No worries."

Melanie looked relieved, and Rafe realized she was probably on a pretty tight budget since her new job likely didn't pay anything near what she'd been making at Ranier Industries. He didn't really understand why she wasn't looking for something better.

As Melanie stepped outside, Rafe behind her, she regretted that this time with him was about to end. The tattoo had been painful, but not as bad as she'd anticipated. It had been so nice, though, having him there to literally hold her hand through it.

"Would you like a ride home?" he asked.

She gazed at him in his jeans and tank top, tattoos visible over his chest and flowing down his arms and she couldn't help laughing. "I just got a mental picture of you dressed just as you are now climbing into that shiny, black limo."

He shrugged. "Sure, why not? Would you like to ride in the limo?"

She had always wanted to. It seemed so glamorous and luxurious. It would be a taste of how the other half lived.

"Or, since it's such a nice day, we could ride my motorcycle."

She raised her eyebrow. "You have a motorcycle?"

"That's right. It's over there." He nodded his head toward a big, gleaming, burgundy Harley parked on the street in front of the shop. "But I know some women are a little intimidated by them."

Melanie laughed. "Not me. I've always wanted to ride one." She walked to the big machine and ran her fingers over the soft, black, leather seat. "I would love to ride with you."

His lips turned up in a devilish grin. "Really?"

She glanced at him and realized her statement might have sounded a little . . . sexual. Suddenly, an image washed through her of straddling Rafe, and slowly moving up and down on him, his big erection buried deep inside her. A wild surge of hormones vibrated through her.

As her cheeks blossomed with heat, she flicked her gaze to the seat again. "Um, yeah. It would be a real adventure. Then I can cross two items off my bucket list—getting a tattoo and riding a motorcycle."

"I never knew you had such a wild side."

Before she could respond, he opened the back compartment and handed her a helmet, then pulled one on himself.

She opened her bag and grabbed the light sweater she'd brought with her and started to pull it on. Ever the gentleman, Rafe grabbed it and held it up for her so she could easily push her arms into the sleeves. As she zipped it up, he pulled a black leather jacket from the storage bin and put it on.

Oh, man, he looked incredibly hot in denim and leather. He mounted the bike and she climbed on behind him.

Once she was settled, he glanced back at her. "You sure you want to go straight home?"

"No, take me for a ride." She smiled.

The big machine roared to life.

"Hold on," he said.

Melanie gazed at the broad shoulders in front of her and wrapped her arms around his waist. Her heart quivered at the feel of his big body so close, then when he took off into traffic, she hung on tight, her body pressed to his solid back.

He swerved around a car that suddenly pulled into traffic and she gasped, a surge of adrenaline shooting through her, but she knew she was safe with Rafe in control.

"You okay?" he asked.

"Yes," she said loudly over the sound of the engine.

Okay? She was in heaven.

Even if she died right now, she'd be a happy woman. For so long, she had dreamed of being close to Rafe, their bodies locked together. And now, riding on the back of his bike with nothing around them but rushing wind gave her the sensation that she was flying.

He turned right and she clung tighter, her cheek pressed against his back. She breathed in the subtle smell of his leather jacket, loving the soft yet masculine feel of it against her skin.

The vibration of the big machine beneath her, coupled with the feel of his big body so close had her whole body quivering with need. Fantasies of him pulling over and sweeping her into his arms, then kissing her silly vibrated through her brain. If he did that, she just knew she'd beg him to take her back to his place and have his way with her.

He slowed down and pulled into a parking space in front of a restaurant with a patio out front. Rectangular planters filled with petunias in vivid pinks, rich purples, and white were affixed to the wrought-iron railing defining the outdoor space. He stopped the engine and, reluctantly, she released his big body, wishing she could hold onto him forever.

He dismounted and pulled off his helmet.

"You like Italian? This place is great, and casual attire is okay."

"It looks lovely, and I adore Italian food."

She pulled off her helmet and he stowed it with his in the hard-shelled compartment on the back of the motorcycle.

As soon as they stepped inside, a man in a suit hurried to greet them.

"Mr. Ranier, my pleasure to see you this evening. Would you like a table on the patio? Or would you prefer to be inside?"

Rafe glanced at her.

"Do you mind if we stay inside?" she asked. "In case it gets cold."

"No problem," the host said. "I have a table right by the window. You'll have a lovely view."

"Thank you, Giorgio." Rafe gestured for Melanie to follow Giorgio as he led them to their table.

True to his word, Giorgio sat them at a table with a view of the street out front and the lovely flowers.

"The chicken marsala is one of our specials tonight. I know how much you enjoy that." Giorgio opened a menu and set it down in front of her, then did the same for Rafe. "Also, Antonio made a special lobster-stuffed ravioli with a rosé sauce."

A waiter placed ice water in front of them, each glass with a twist of lemon, then continued on his way.

"Lobster ravioli?" Melanie smiled. "That sounds delicious."

"Two raviolis it is, and a carafe of the house wine." Rafe closed his menu and handed it to Giorgio.

"Excellent." Giorgio scooped up her menu and hurried away.

Melanie picked up the cloth napkin and laid it on her lap. When she glanced up again, Rafe's sky blue gaze was upon her. She sipped her water, not quite sure what to do with herself.

"This is kind of strange," she said finally.

His eyebrows hiked up. "What is?"

"Sitting here with you. In a restaurant."

"We've been out for meals together before."

"Yeah, sure. At Christmas. Usually with a couple of the other staff."

"And on your birthday."

It was true. He'd always been very considerate that way.

"But you were my boss. This is different."

He smiled. "That's right. Now it's as friends."

She had to stop her smile from fading. Friends. Great. He'd gone from being her boss to being her friend. Not really what she'd been hoping for.

"We can be friends, can't we?" he asked.

"Of course. I'd like that."

"Good."

The waiter brought the carafe of wine and filled their glasses.

"So are you enjoying being back?" she asked.

After Rafe's father had died, Rafe had left Philadelphia and disappeared for almost a year. Their overbearing father had pushed Rafe to follow in his footsteps, heedless of what Rafe wanted, and once the man was gone, Rafe had needed to get away and discover who he really was. So he'd left Ranier Industries and pursued his dream of being a guitarist in a rock band, and right now, with his faded jeans and tattoos, he looked every bit the part.

Melanie could just picture crowds of women swooning when he came on stage.

"Do you miss it?" Melanie asked. "The rock star lifestyle, I mean."

"I enjoyed being on the road, but it made me realize that despite my difficulties with my father, I really do care about the company. It's the Ranier legacy, and it employs a lot of great people. Since I've been back, I've been doing more to develop green technologies, which has always been a passion of mine. And I'm pleased with all the positive changes Dane has made. The only thing that's hard to get used to is the rigid schedule."

"Well, you're the boss. You can keep your own hours."

"To an extent. But on the whole, business still needs to be done during business hours."

She understood what he meant. He could come in late if he wanted, and leave early, but a lot of what he did involved meeting with other people, and that mostly had to be done during the regular business day.

"Remember, during the past year, I've been playing with a band, and the hours are quite different."

"Well, you could always set a schedule where you only spend a few days in the office and take all your appointments on those days only. Then the other days are your own. Maybe you could play guitar somewhere local. Even a club out of town, if you want to reduce the chance of Ranier employees running into you as Storm."

He smiled. "You know me so well. I've already started looking into pulling together a band and playing at some clubs, but I hadn't thought of concentrating my office hours into a few days."

She smiled. "That's why you love me." As soon as she'd said the words, her gaze darted to his face.

He chuckled. "Yes, I do."

It was something he used to say when he would praise her after she offered a creative solution to a problem he'd been struggling with. It had actually started with him telling her he loved having her as his secretary, then eventually he'd shortened it to *that's why I love you.*

She knew he hadn't really meant it, of course, other than in an affectionate way, but it had still thrilled her every time he'd said it.

God, she was pathetic.

Their dinner arrived, and she picked up her fork and took a bite. The lobster-filled pasta and smooth, creamy sauce melted in her mouth.

"You know, that's why I really wish you'd come back. I miss working with you."

She compressed her lips. "Rafe, I already told you—"

He raised his hands. "I know. I'm sorry. You already know the offer's out there if you want to come back."

She nodded and took another bite. Then she gazed at him again. "But I won't, you know." She put down her fork. "And it's because of you."

His gaze shot to hers and he tilted his head in question.

"I just really admire what you did. You took a risk and walked away. You were living a life someone else had set out for you and instead of just accepting it, you decided to pursue your dream. And to figure out who you really are."

"I'm not sure I've really succeeded."

"Yes, you have. Or at least, you're on the right path." She sipped her wine. "And that inspired me to do the same. I'm not like you. I don't know what I have a passion for—yet—but I do know that I want to be free of rules, and as you said, the nine-to-five existence."

"Did I have too many rules?" he asked.

"No, they were mine. I always behaved the way I was expected to behave. I conformed to what my family wanted, and what society expected. I never really took the time to decide what *I* wanted. So now, with the generous severance Mr. Ranier gave me, I have the opportunity to figure it out."

"So you're working at a coffee shop."

"I don't intend to be defined by my job. That's just what I do to make money. But working there means I have variable hours and some mornings free, and it's the perfect time to paint and sketch—something I never had time for in the corporate world. I want to shake up my life, try new things, and question everything. Seeing what you did inspired me."

He smiled. "I'm glad. So what else do you want to do?"

"I don't know. Maybe meet a handsome guy and do something really wild and crazy."

His lips turned up in a grin. "You mean in the bedroom?"

"Oh, uh . . ." Ever since Jessica had told her a little about how exciting she found it to be dominated in the bedroom, Melanie had dreamed of trying that herself, but she hadn't meant to let that slip.

She glanced at him and his eyes twinkled with mischief. Her cheeks flushed hotly.

"I just meant we wouldn't do the same old boring things." This was not making it better. "You know, like dates where we go to the movies or whatever."

As he gazed at her speculatively, she stared at her wineglass, wrapping her fingers around the stem.

"I don't intend to fall into old patterns," she continued. "I want to push the limits on everything I do. At least, for a while."

She took the conversation back to her art, and before long, the waiter took away their empty plates, offered dessert, which they declined, and the bill arrived. They stepped out into the warm evening air and walked toward his big motorcycle.

"May I give you a ride home?"

"Thank you. I'd like that."

She climbed onto the big machine behind him and they sped across the city to her apartment building. Too soon he pulled up in front of the entrance and got off the bike, then retrieved her bag from the storage container and walked her to the glass door.

"Thanks again for dinner. And the ride home." She opened her purse and pulled out her key. She gazed up at him. "And I really appreciate you staying with me while I got the tattoo."

"It was my pleasure. You know, today I saw a whole new side of you, and I found it very intriguing." He smiled warmly. "I'd really like the opportunity to get to know you better."

She gazed at his handsome face, mesmerized by his twinkling, sky blue eyes, and returned his smile. "I'd like that."

She longed to reach up and stroke his spiky, dark hair.

They stood in silence for a few seconds and she realized he was waiting for her to open her door.

It had been a wonderful evening and she didn't want it to end, but she was sure as soon as she opened her door, he would say good night and be gone.

"I . . . uh . . . do you think it was a good choice? The tattoo I mean?"

"Yours or mine?"

"Yours is gorgeous," she said. "Do you think mine looks as nice?"

"Yours is beautiful. I can't believe I didn't know you had such artistic ability. And you said it represents freedom. Because you're spreading your wings?"

She nodded. "Freedom and happiness. The bluebird of happiness taking flight."

He smiled. "I like that. And I like that I got to see the tattoo that only a few special men will ever see."

The warmth in his eyes sent a quiver through her. It had been embarrassing pulling down her top to reveal her breast with Rafe there. And exciting at the same time.

"Along with the stranger who put it there," she said.

Oh, man, why had she ruined the mood by saying that?

He laughed. "I guess that's true."

"Um . . ." She gazed up at him. "Do you want to come up and see it again?"

As soon as the words left her mouth, she thought she'd die. How could she say that?

Their gazes locked, and he hesitated.

"Oh, God, I shouldn't have said that." She stuffed her key into the lock and turned it, then pulled open the door. "I didn't mean it the way it sounded." Of course, she had meant it exactly the way it sounded, but his hesitation had spoken volumes.

The uncertainty in his eyes prompted her to continue. "It's just that I've never had a tattoo before and . . . well, I'm just being silly wanting you to look at it when I take the dressing off. I'm sure it's fine."

"If you're really concerned—"

"No, really. It's fine. Thanks anyway."

Oh, God, was he really buying that? But she definitely didn't want him to come up now. It would be so awkward.

He smiled. "I enjoyed today. Thank you." He tucked his finger under her chin and tipped her face up, sending tingles through her. His lips brushed hers in the barest whisper of a kiss, and she thought she'd faint.

This was how fantasies were born.

Then he stepped back. "Good night."

She nodded, then slipped in the door, glancing over her shoulder as she walked across the lobby. He waited outside the door until she turned down the corridor to the elevator before he walked away.

Rafe ensured Melanie got inside okay, then lingered as he watched her walk across the lobby.

What the hell was that? And now he couldn't drag his gaze from her delightfully swaying derriere. It looked so round and inviting in those snug jeans of hers.

Memories of the creamy swell of her breast, the virginal flesh exposed and ready for her tattoo, lingered in his mind. Ever since Charlie had covered it with the dressing, Rafe couldn't stop thinking about it. Couldn't stop *longing* to touch it.

If it had been any other woman, he would have flirted all through dinner, then suggested they go back to his place. Or hers. But when Melanie had invited him up to her place . . . to see the damned tattoo, no less . . . he had faltered.

She had denied coming on to him, but she couldn't hide the need in her eyes.

So why had he held back?

He flipped open the storage compartment on his bike and pulled out his helmet. There were times they'd worked long hours together, and he couldn't help but notice that hot little body she kept well hidden behind her conservative business attire. But he'd cared about her too much to jeopardize their working relationship.

So he'd suppressed his attraction to her. And with great success. He was sure neither Melanie, Dane, nor anyone else knew he could barely contain himself when she was near. He'd become such a master at controlling those feelings, he'd almost forgotten about them.

Almost.

But today . . . fuck, his groin ached with need.

As he pulled on the helmet and fastened it, he noticed something sitting in the bottom of the container, beside the helmet Melanie had worn.

Ah, damn it.

———

Melanie stepped off the elevator, then walked down the hall to her apartment. Once inside, she closed the door behind her, then leaned against it.

Now, if only she could forget the whole embarrassing incident downstairs. She cringed at the thought of her lame come-on, then the way she'd babbled in an attempt to deny it. He'd probably seen right through her excuse.

She unzipped her sweater and tugged it off, then tossed it over the back of the couch.

"I'm such a dumbass," she muttered as she walked into her bathroom and gazed in the mirror at the white patch on her chest. She was happy to distract herself by pulling off her top and gently peeling the dressing away, exposing the beautiful tattoo. The artist had done a wonderful job. She touched the reddened flesh around the design. It felt slick. She grabbed a fresh washcloth and dampened it, then wiped over the tattoo, as per the instructions they'd sent with her. Then she reached for the small tube of ointment from her dresser and applied it.

A knock sounded on her door. She pulled on her top again, then straightened it and hurried to the entrance. She smiled, assuming it was Jessica, coming over to see her new ink.

Oh, man, thank heavens Rafe hadn't come up after all. It would have been awkward if Jessica had arrived with Rafe here.

Especially since as soon as the man walked into her apartment, she probably would have thrown herself at him and torn off his clothes.

She grabbed the doorknob, anxious to show Jessica her new tattoo. When she pulled it open, shock vaulted through her.

There in the doorway stood big, sexy Rafe, a crooked smile on his face.

Savage Kiss

Melanie's heart skipped a beat as she stared at the wick-edly sexy Rafe, his large frame filling her doorway.

"Uh . . . hi," she stammered. "Come in."

With his broad shoulders and tattoos flowing down his muscular arms, he could be an intimidating presence. In fact, she was amazed someone actually let him in the front door, but then, who would argue with him?

A shiver danced down her spine as he stepped inside. Big and utterly masculine, he seemed to take up all the space in her tiny apartment. Something she'd dreamed of for a long time.

"Sorry to just show up at your door, but your wallet fell out of your bag," he said. "I found it in the storage compartment when I went to grab my helmet."

He held it out to her, and she almost giggled at the sight of her bright pink, rhinestone-adorned wallet in his big, masculine hand.

Oh, damn, she was giddy.

She took it from him, trying to ignore the shiver of heat that rushed along her arm at the brush of his fingers against hers.

"I'm glad you found it. I would have panicked tomorrow morning when I noticed it was missing. Plus, it has my bus pass."

She grabbed her purse and slid the wallet inside, then closed the snap, which was a little flakey. That's why the darned wallet had fallen out. Not that she was complaining. It gave her another chance to see Rafe.

"So how's your tattoo?" he asked. "I see you've taken off the dressing."

Her hand fluttered to her breast as she turned to face him again. "Oh, it's fine. Just a little red, which they said to expect."

His gaze slid to her breast, and she couldn't push away the memory of her earlier suggestion that he come up and check it out. Now, with him here, she was tempted to draw down the fabric of her top to reveal the tattoo to him. And more.

"Okay. I guess I'll be on my way."

"Wait," she said. "Would you like coffee? I have decaf. Or soda? Or beer?"

His lips turned up in a charming smile. "I'd like that. A soda will be fine."

She went into the kitchen and filled two glasses with cola, then returned to the living room to find him sitting on the couch. She handed him one and sat down beside him.

"Did you do that?" he asked, gazing at the sketch of a

phoenix she'd framed and hung on the wall over the desk.

"Yes, how did you know?"

"It's the same style as your tattoo." He nodded toward the phoenix. "It's very good. Have you tried selling your art?"

She placed her glass on the coffee table. "Oh, no. I mean, sometimes a friend will ask me to do something for them, but I never charge them."

"You know, if you're interested in doing something artistic for a living, I'm sure we could find something for you in the art department at Ranier Industries."

She smiled. "There you go trying to help me out again. You know, you're not responsible for me."

"You're right, but I'd like to help. Not because I feel obligated. I think you're talented and just need a chance to shine. I'd love to help you do that."

"Did you want help when you broke away from the company and went off on your motorcycle to find your-self?"

His lips quirked up. "No, but I have a big bank account to fall back on. And the family business. You have to play it closer to the edge. But I get it. You want to do it on your own."

She smiled and took a sip of her drink. "Talking about your time away, how was it playing your guitar in front of huge audiences?"

His eyes glowed. "It was a pure adrenaline rush."

She grinned. "A few months ago, I never would have

been able to imagine Rafe Ranier, businessman, always impeccably dressed in a designer suit, playing guitar with a rock band in front of screaming fans, but after seeing you with your tattoos and leather jacket, and riding the big motorcycle . . ." She shrugged. "I still say you inspire me."

He leaned forward. "I like that." The intensity of his gaze unsettled her. "If I can be some part of you breaking free and finding yourself, that makes me feel good."

She gazed into his sky blue eyes, her heartbeat increasing. "I'm glad I make you feel good."

He was so close. With his broad shoulders and impressive height, she felt tiny in comparison. She felt the pull of his masculinity as she leaned a little closer. Heat simmered in his eyes as his face drew nearer, then he tipped up her chin. Her breath held as his lips brushed hers. Lightly. Tenderly. Then his mouth moved on hers. She breathed in his musky male scent mixed with leather and mint. The tip of his tongue teased her lips and she opened. Her arms swept around his neck as he slid into her mouth. His hands glided around her waist and he drew her closer. Her eyelids fell closed as she felt his arms envelop her.

Oh, God, this was really happening. She was in Rafe Ranier's arms. They were alone in her apartment and he was kissing her. Her bedroom was only yards away. She curled her tongue around his and stroked it. Weak with need, she melted against him.

His mouth drew away and she opened her eyes.

He seemed uncertain. "Melanie, are you sure—"

A knock sounded on the door and she jumped. Rafe drew away and she mentally cursed whoever it was.

"We could wait until they go away," Melanie suggested, but then another knock sounded.

"Melanie, it's Jessica."

"Coming," Melanie called, then her gaze shot to Rafe. "Will this be awkward for you?"

"Don't worry about it."

She stood up and walked to the door. Maybe *he* wouldn't find it awkward, but Melanie wasn't too happy about Jessica finding Melanie and Rafe alone in her apartment.

Not that Jessica would mind. She'd done everything she could to encourage Melanie to start a relationship with Rafe.

She opened the door and Jessica smiled at her.

"So let's see that tattoo," Jessica said as she stepped in the room. Then she stopped. "Rafe, hi." She glanced back at Melanie and smiled. "I can come back another time if I'm interrupting."

Rafe stood up. "Not at all. Melanie and I ran into each other at the tattoo studio and grabbed dinner together."

"Then he found I left my wallet behind and he brought it up," Melanie added.

"And now I'm going to take off." Rafe walked toward the door.

"I'll see you at the office Monday?" Jessica asked.

"The staff meeting at ten. I'll be there." Then he disappeared out the door.

Jessica stared at Melanie with a Cheshire Cat smile. "So . . . do I sense romance in the air?"

Melanie narrowed her eyes. "Did you have anything to do with us meeting today?"

"What do you mean?" Jessica asked innocently.

"You said someone recommended the studio. I assume that was Rafe. And did you by chance arrange my appointment right after his?"

"I may have found out he was going in for another tattoo, and happened to book the same day." But Jessica couldn't keep a straight face under Melanie's stare. She laughed. "Okay, you caught me. But it worked, didn't it? It triggered your first date with Rafe."

"It wasn't a date. It was just dinner."

"Did he kiss you?"

Melanie frowned. "You know, you're entirely too nosy."

Jessica laughed again. "Okay, fine. Now let's see that ink."

The bell over the shop door jingled as Melanie finished lining up the muffins in the display case.

"Wowza!" Sue whispered. "If you don't hit that, you're crazy."

Melanie stood up to see Rafe, impeccably dressed in a dark gray suit, dove-gray shirt, and dark teal and charcoal tie walking toward her. He was a stunning sight.

And other than the subtle glint of the diamond studs in his ears, there was no hint of the laid-back biker with arms and chest adorned with tattoos. He looked every bit the wealthy businessman.

She smiled. "What can I get you?" she asked, trying not to think about his arms around her, his tongue gliding into her mouth. And how warm and solid his body felt against hers.

"Nothing. I just wanted to talk for a minute," he said. "Do you have time?"

The place was empty. "Uh . . . yes. Of course." She knew Sue wouldn't mind covering for her, just like she did when Sue's sister came in.

She followed him to the same table they'd sat at last time, near the back, then sat down.

"I just wanted to make sure we're okay after Saturday night," he began.

She blinked. She was okay with what had happened. More than okay. But it sounded like he wasn't.

"Um . . . sure. Why wouldn't I be?"

"It's just . . . things were getting pretty hot and heavy."

"Is there anything wrong with that?"

"I just don't want to jeopardize our friendship."

She shrugged, but she could feel her cheeks heating in embarrassment. She'd thought the attraction was mutual, but he must have just been caught up in a rush of hormones. Clearly it wasn't her he'd been attracted to. Just any woman would have sufficed, and Melanie had made it clear she'd be ready and willing.

"Okay. No harm done. I don't know what either of

us was thinking." She tried to laugh casually, but it came out strangled and sad. She stood up. "I should get back to work." She turned to escape.

"Wait."

She turned back. His brow creased and his blue eyes were filled with concern.

"I seem to have insulted you and I didn't mean that. Melanie, this is new territory for us. I just don't want to ruin things."

"What is it you do want?" she asked point-blank.

He stood up and pulled something from his inside jacket pocket and handed it to her. She glanced down at it. A ticket to an event.

"I'm playing with Savage Kiss at an outdoor concert on Saturday. You said you'd like to see me play sometime. What I want is for you to come to the concert."

Saturday was a hot day, so Melanie decided to wear a camisole and a short denim skirt. She tossed a light sweater in her large shoulder bag and went down to the lobby of her building.

The concert was about an hour out of town, so Rafe had offered to send a car for her. She'd be meeting him after the show.

When she walked out the door, she saw a black limo waiting at the curb, the chauffeur standing beside it.

"Ms. Taylor?"

"Yes."

He opened the door and she climbed inside.

She sat back in the ultra-comfortable leather seat and

glanced around. There was a bar along the side with small bottles of wine, cans of soda, beer, and juice. There were nuts, chips, and other snacks, too. On the right was a TV.

Wow. This was luxury. She could happily relax and fall asleep in this seat.

The car pulled smoothly from the curb. She poured a glass of wine and turned on the TV, then relaxed. The miles and minutes just seemed to slip by as she sipped the rich Cabernet. When they finally arrived at the venue, she thanked the driver and followed the other people flocking to the admission gate, her ticket at the ready.

Once she was inside, a uniformed security guard walked toward her.

"Good evening, miss. Are you Melanie Taylor?"

"Yes." She reached into her purse to find the ticket stub and pulled it out.

"Come with me."

Her chest compressed. "Is something wrong?"

He smiled. "Not at all." But he gave no further explanation.

He led her through the crowd, toward the stage, then to a cordoned-off VIP area where a few other people were sitting on cushioned folding chairs. Outside the select area, people stood or sat on blankets.

Once she sat down, another security person set down a black bag beside her chair. It looked like a soft-sided cooler.

"This is for you." He handed her an envelope, then the two of them went on their way.

She opened the envelope and in Rafe's familiar hand-writing it said, "Enjoy the show."

She opened the zipper on the bag and inside were several bottles of a vodka drink she hadn't tried before, but some were mango and berry so she knew she'd like them. Also, there were a couple of bottles of water and some bags of nuts and chips.

It was like being on a date but without her date present.

She opened a bottle and sat back. Before long, the band was introduced and excitement murmured through the crowd. The members of Savage Kiss bounded onto stage, and the crowd cheered. One band member stepped forward, introducing himself as Travis.

Making use of visual effects, Travis expertly whipped the crowd's enthusiasm to a frenzy of excitement as he introduced each band member. Storm came last, appearing out of an explosion of smoke and a blaze of lights.

Women cheered wildly at the sight of him. And Melanie couldn't blame them. He wore a black tank top that showed off his muscular, tattooed arms, and he oozed the aura of a sexy bad boy who set any woman to dreaming of wicked nights in his arms.

When he began to play his guitar solo, Melanie's eyes widened. My God, he was talented. And his charisma on stage was captivating.

She sat mesmerized for the entire show, trying to reconcile this wild performer with the Rafe she knew.

After they'd played their final set, the crowd cheered and applauded until the band came out for an encore.

Even after that, the enthusiasm of the crowd was relentless. People even started calling for Storm until he came out and performed a final solo. Anticipation quivered through her as she realized she'd soon be with him. Just the two of them.

At least, she assumed he'd be meeting her after the show. But she wasn't sure how to go about getting backstage to see him, and she doubted that he'd come into the crowd to find her. He'd be mobbed.

Finally, the show was well and truly over and the crowd started to break up. She left the VIP area and meandered toward the stage. Other women were gathering by the fenced-off area and security guards hovered around.

She waited with the other women, unsure what to do. After about twenty minutes, she began to despair that she'd misread the situation. But surely Rafe wouldn't leave her stranded this far from the city. Maybe the limo driver was waiting for her where he'd dropped her off. She turned with a sigh and started walking toward the entrance.

"I think he's coming," a woman said excitedly.

"Over there. Isn't that him?" another woman cried.

As Melanie turned toward the fence again, several women started to shriek and wave.

"Storm! Over here!"

Melanie was still near the front of the crowd and was pushed toward the fence as the women surged toward it. Melanie grasped the linked metal as she peered through to the other side.

There was Storm, walking in their direction.

"Hello, ladies." He smiled as he continued toward them.

"Oh, Storm, we love you!" a woman screamed.

"Storm, I want you so bad," another said.

"I'll show you a good time you'll never forget," a third yelled, then lifted her top and revealed her bare breasts. Her enormous, perfectly formed breasts.

"Me, too," responded another and she pulled up her top, too.

Soon several pairs of bare breasts peered toward him. He smiled and stopped about a yard from the fence, glancing across the crowd.

The brashness of the women shocked Melanie, but it was also exciting and wild.

Just then, Storm's gaze turned to her and recognition flickered in his eyes.

She locked gazes with him, then obeyed the urge thrumming through her, and reached for the hem of her camisole top, then tugged it up, revealing her naked breasts.

They might not be as spectacular as the first woman's, or as big and round as the others', but Storm's eyes lit up at the sight of them.

Within seconds, someone grasped her shoulder and she glanced behind her. A big, burly security guard frowned at her. She tugged down her top.

"Come with me, miss."

She glanced at the guard's stern face and her cheeks heated with embarrassment. Oh, God, was she being arrested for indecent exposure? Oh, damn, why had she listened to that wild, erratic voice in her head?

In the commotion of the crowd, she lost sight of Storm. The guard led her through the crowd, past the stage, toward a tent with a sign stating SECURITY.

As they neared the security tent, however, Melanie's guard veered to the side and took her to a gate in the fence. It was wooden, blocking the view of what was behind it.

They stepped through the gate and it closed behind her. On the other side of the fence the bright lights that had turned on after the show so that people could see their way out were still blazing, but it was shadowy here. She gazed around, disoriented. Someone stepped toward her.

"There you are." Storm grinned at her.

Her guard escort released her arm and disappeared through the gate again, leaving her standing alone with Storm.

"I thought they were going to arrest me."

"For flashing me?" He chuckled. "That happens all the time. One of the hazards of the job."

He stepped toward her and tucked his finger under her chin, then tipped it up. "You are becoming quite the naughty vixen, aren't you? I never would have thought you'd do something like that."

Her cheeks flushed, but thankfully he wouldn't be able to see them in the dim light.

He turned and started to walk along the paved path and she walked alongside him, as they made their way through the small private lot behind the concert hall.

There was only space for about fifteen cars, and none of the other people with access were mulling about just yet.

"I guess I got caught up in the excitement."

He grinned. "Well, I certainly found it pretty exciting."

"Seeing all those bare breasts, you mean?" she said.

He stopped and turned toward her. "No. Seeing your beautiful bare breasts."

She stared up at his glittering eyes and couldn't help herself. She grasped his broad shoulders and pushed herself onto her tiptoes, then kissed him.

His arms swept around her and he tugged her close to his body, then his tongue slid into her mouth and gently explored. She groaned and held him tighter, her breasts crushed against his solid chest.

"Fuck, Melanie," he ground out.

Heat thrummed through her and she glanced around, then grasped his hand and guided him off the path and into the shadow of the trees.

"We can go to my trailer," he suggested as she pulled him along.

She tugged him behind a big tree. "I like it here."

Then she grabbed the hem of her top and pulled it up, revealing her breasts once again.

"I can't see you here." His words came out low and hoarse.

He shifted her a little to the right, still away from where anyone would see them, but where the moonlight filtered through the leaves. She could see his face as he gazed down at her breasts, his eyes blazing with heat.

She took his hand and raised it to her chest, then placed it over her naked breast. His fingers curled around her, cupping her, her hardened nipple pressing into his palm.

His gaze met hers and there was a ferocity in his blue eyes she'd never seen before.

Then she stroked over the bulge in his jeans and he groaned softly. He took his hand off her breast and grasped her wrist, but he didn't pull her hand away.

"I want you," she murmured. "I have for a long time."

"Fuck, I'm going to wind up taking you right against the tree if we keep this up."

Excitement flashed through her. "Yes. Do it."

She sucked in a breath as he surged forward, backing her up against the wide trunk. He tugged off her top then kissed her neck, pressing her bare back against the rough bark. Then his lips found hers again and he stormed her mouth, his body pressing her hard against the tree.

"Oh, Storm," she breathed against his ear. "I want to feel you inside me."

He nipped her ear. "I want to take it slow. To explore every inch of you."

"Later," she murmured. "Right now, I want you to fuck me hard against this tree." She stroked down his chest, over his tight abs, then wrapped her fingers around his denim-covered erection.

"Please," she moaned, then nipped his lower lip.

"Fuck, Melanie." He pressed her back against the tree again, then unzipped his pants and pulled out his cock.

She curled her fingers around his hot shaft and stroked. God, he was enormous. Her fingers couldn't wrap all the way around him. He found the hem of her short denim skirt and tugged it up. She stroked his erection, up and down, and he moaned against her ear.

"At this rate, I won't last long."

She giggled, loving the power she had over him.

His fingers brushed her inner thigh, then traveled up and swept across the lace covering her mound.

"Fuck, you're wet. I can feel it through your panties."

Then he tugged the fabric aside and slid his fingertip over her slick swollen flesh.

His touch sent a rush of molten desire straight through her, and she gasped for breath.

His fingers slipped away, then she felt something hard and hot pressing against her.

He nipped her earlobe hard, sending heat thrumming through her.

"You want me." He pushed against her, the tip of his hot cock dipping into her.

"Oh, yes," she breathed.

"Tell me again," he insisted.

"I want you inside me. I want you to fuck me hard."

He eased forward, his cockhead stretching her. Exquisite delight shimmered through her.

She clung to his shoulders. "Deeper. Fill me up."

As he pushed inside, his big, welcome cock sliding deeper, she moaned at the exquisite stretching sensation.

She'd longed for this for so long, and it was better than she'd ever imagined.

He surged forward, his cock driving all the way in, pinning her to the tree.

"I love your hot pussy so tight around me." He captured her mouth and plunged his tongue into her in deep thrusts until she gasped for air. "Now I'm going to fuck you so hard, you'll never forget this first time."

He grasped her wrists and pushed them over her head, then drew back, his big cockhead stroking her inner passage. He drove deep again.

She pressed against his grip, moaning in delight.

He drew back and thrust, back and thrust, back and thrust. Joy swelled through her as he continued to fill her like a piston, pulsing deep into her over and over.

"Oh, yes. I'm—" she sucked in a breath "—so close."

"Me, too, baby." He picked up speed and she gasped at the potent pleasure pummeling her.

Then he thrust hard, pinning her to the tree again and she felt him pulse inside her. The feel of his liquid heat filling her sent her over the edge. She moaned, arching against him as pleasure spiraled through her. He began to move again, filling her with his hard length. She pushed against his restraining hand and moaned, then exploded in orgasm. Bliss washed through her as she moaned into his ear.

Finally, she relaxed, collapsing against his big, strong body. He released her wrists and his arms enveloped her as she listened to his accelerated heartbeat. She luxuriated in his nearness.

He kissed her ear, then drew back. His eyes glowed as he gazed at her.

"Melanie, that was incredible." A glint of uncertainty flashed in his eyes. "Are you sure you're okay with . . . what just happened?"

She just smiled, and he leaned in and kissed her again.

"Good." He grinned. "I was going to take you to meet the rest of the band, but if you get that excited around all musicians, I'm not sure I should." He leaned in close and nuzzled her temple. "I don't want to share you."

She stroked over his shoulders. "It's only you who excites me like that."

As he stared at her, his smile faded and he drew her close and kissed her again.

"I know a nice hotel not far from here. Instead of going back to the city tonight, let's get a room."

She just nodded, while her heart quivered in anticipation. The thought of spending the night with Rafe, cocooned in a soft bed with his arms around her, filled her with joy.

Once they straightened their clothes, he took her hand and led her back to the path, then to the parking lot. She held his big hand tight, loving the feel of his warm fingers enveloping hers. As they approached his bike, heat coiled through her at the thought of the two of them climbing into a big warm bed together, then him prowling over her and—

"Hey, Storm. Diego and I are headed out for a drink. Want to join us?" The tall, sandy-haired man smiled at her, a twinkle in his blue-green eyes. "Your friend can come, too."

She recognized him as the lead singer of Savage Kiss,

and the one who had introduced the band. The other was the drummer, who'd had a wicked solo near the end that had left her breathless. Both had on faded jeans, and Diego wore a black leather vest with silver studs while Travis wore a long-sleeved charcoal T-shirt. Diego's thick black hair was cropped short but what there was rose in spikes, while Travis had longish, unkempt sandy hair that was parted on the side and tapered, brushing his collar at the back. Travis was taller than Diego by about five inches, but both were muscular, and sexy as sin.

A shiver danced through her and she realized she was a little starstruck by these men. Both had killer smiles, and a glimmer in their eyes like they were looking for trouble, and just might have found it.

Oh, God, could they tell that she and Storm had just had sex? Had they *seen* them? Her cheeks heated, but she realized she was just being silly.

"This is Travis and Diego," Rafe said. "And this is Melanie."

"Melanie?" Travis smiled and offered his hand.

When she shook it, he held hers in a tight grip.

"You're the one who helped my sister, Jess, when she moved to Philly."

"You're Jessica's brother? It's nice to meet you."

Melanie hadn't realized that Savage Kiss was the band Rafe had been a part of back in Bakersfield when he'd met Jessica.

"Jess really appreciated your help. She worried about leaving Bakersfield, but it helped that she found a close friend so soon. Thanks for helping out my baby sister."

"It was my pleasure. I love Jessica."

"We have something in common then." He grinned and drew her hand to his elbow, then tucked it around his arm. "You can't say no to a drink now."

She glanced helplessly over her shoulder at Storm as Travis led her across the parking lot.

"Hell, no. You're not stealing my girl." Storm strode after them and grasped her other arm.

Her stomach clenched. Were they going to fight over her?

But Travis just laughed. "I could if I wanted to, man." He winked at Melanie as he let her go. "Meet us over at The Saloon. Same place as last night."

She followed Storm to his bike, then pulled on the helmet he handed her. He fastened the clasp under her chin and then drew her in for a deep kiss. "Just remember, you're mine." Then he winked and mounted the bike.

Was he really jealous, she wondered as she wrapped her arms around his waist? Or just teasing her? The bike roared to life and fifteen minutes later they pulled up in front of a rustic tavern with a sign that read THE SALOON.

When they stepped inside, they saw Diego and Travis already at a solid wooden table, with four dark beers in glass steins in front of them. They sat down and Storm grabbed one, then took a deep sip.

"Maybe Melanie doesn't want a beer," Storm said.

Travis grabbed the handle of Storm's beer and pulled it toward himself. "Those are our beers. Get your own, you mooch."

Melanie pushed the beer in front of her toward Diego, but they all broke out laughing.

"It's okay, *belleza,*" Diego said in a sexy Spanish accent as he pushed the beer toward her again. "They always kid around like that. Do you want me to get you something else?"

His dark brown eyes glowed warmly as he smiled at her, sending shivers down her spine.

"No, this is fine, thanks." She wrapped her hand around the cold glass handle and took a sip. "Mm. This is good." She liked the deep, rich flavor of the dark beer.

"So Jess tells me you work for my future brother-in-law," Travis said.

Melanie glanced at Storm, who just sipped his beer. Did Travis not know that Storm was really billionaire business mogul Rafe Ranier, and that Dane and Rafe were related?

"I did, but I quit recently. I'm working as a barista now."

"You left a job in a big company to work in a coffee place?" Diego asked. "Your boss drive you to quit or something?"

His raised eyebrows indicated he was kidding, but Melanie's stomach churned at just how close he'd come to the truth. She shrugged, trying to keep her expression neutral. "I wanted more freedom."

"Freedom?" Diego chuckled. "Like freedom to be broke?"

Her cheeks heated and she stared at her beer.

"Sorry, *belleza,* I didn't mean to make fun. I'm just trying to understand you better. There must be a reason you gave up benefits and a good salary for this freedom."

She nodded. "Well, just like you, I want to do what I'm passionate about."

His eyebrows arched. "And you're passionate about coffee?"

"No. I'm still trying to figure it out. But I knew I didn't want to be confined by the rules of an office job anymore. I got restless and needed a change." She shrugged. "I might take some classes, or maybe do some traveling." She shook her head. "I don't know yet. I just wanted to get out of the same old routine and experience new things."

"Actually, she's quite an artist," Storm said. "And she wants to live a little more on the edge. She even designed her own tattoo."

"Can we see it?" Travis asked.

"Afraid not, boys," Storm said. "Only a special few get to see that one."

Diego grinned. "And you're one of them?"

Travis laughed. "And the thousand other people standing around when she flashed him."

Her gaze shot to his as her cheeks blazed with heat. "There weren't a thousand."

Diego and Travis both chuckled.

"Maybe not," Travis said, "but Diego and I got a quick peek from where we were standing helping the crew." He winked. "Nice. I didn't really get to see much of the tattoo, though." He grinned. "Maybe sometime I'll get a better look."

Storm said nothing, but she could sense the tension in him. He drained his glass. "You almost finished?"

She glanced down at her mug, still half full, then took a big sip and pushed it aside. "I'm good." She smiled at Diego and Travis. "Thanks for inviting me along."

"Anytime," Travis said.

Diego took her hand and kissed the back of it. "Our pleasure, *belleza*."

She followed Storm out the front door toward the parking lot. At his scowling face, she frowned.

"Are you mad at me?"

He glanced at her. "No, of course not."

"You don't seem very happy."

He took her hand and pulled her into his arms for a kiss. "Sorry. I guess I got a bit jealous back there. Travis and I are good friends, but if he could steal you away, he would. It's just a weird rivalry that started between us when we were on the road."

"After you dumped his sister? Maybe he was trying to prevent you from moving on in hopes you'd go back to her."

Storm shrugged. "Maybe. Or maybe he wants to punish me. But even though she's hooked up with Dane now, I don't think it's changed between Travis and me." He stormed her lips again. "And I want to keep you for myself."

Her heart thundered in her chest at the passion of his

kiss and she sighed when he released her lips. Then they continued to walk.

"I'm surprised that Travis doesn't know you're Dane's brother," she said.

"This week is the first time I've seen him since I left the band. I just haven't mentioned it yet."

She gazed at him. "Are you sure that's all it is?"

Storm shrugged. "It'll be strange when they find out I'm Rafe Ranier, owner of Ranier Industries. It's not really consistent with the image they have of Storm."

"You'll have to tell them sometime. Her brother, at least, will be at the wedding."

He opened the storage compartment on the back of the bike.

"I'll figure that out later." His eyes glittered as he gazed at her, sending heat thrumming through her. "Right now, I just want to get you into that hotel room."

He handed her a helmet and she climbed on the back of his bike. Within moments, they were on the road.

The vibration of the bike between her legs and the heat and hardness of his body tight against her had her almost panting when they pulled up in front of the hotel.

The stone building looked very elegant, with tall columns at the entrance, beautiful arches, and detailed stonework. When they stepped inside, she drew in a breath. Shiny marble floors, carved columns, high ceilings with crystal chandeliers, and scattered sitting areas of supple leather couches and glass tables all added to the elegance of the huge lobby. She breathed in the lovely scent from a huge floral arrangement they passed as Storm led her to the reception desk.

The man they approached watched them with disapproval in his eyes. Melanie glanced around and realized that their attire did not fit with that of the more upscale guests moving through the grand space.

"I'd like a room," Storm said.

The man pursed his lips. "I don't believe we have anything available, sir." The man hadn't even glanced at his computer screen.

Storm's eyebrow arched. "Really? If you don't have any rooms, then how about a suite?"

"I'm sorry, sir. All we have is the Presidential Suite and that's fifteen hundred dollars a night."

"I'll take it." He tossed his credit card on the counter and the man picked it up reluctantly.

When he saw the card, he seemed to deflate. Clearly, he recognized the name. "Oh, Mr. Ranier, I am so sorry. I didn't realize . . ." His cheeks tinged with red as he tapped on his keyboard. "Would you like me to have a bellman collect your luggage?"

"No luggage. We'll just be staying the one night."

"Very good, sir." He handed Storm a keycard. "If there's anything you need, let us know."

"Just make sure we're not disturbed." He winked at Melanie as they stepped away from the desk.

Melanie felt totally conspicuous in her denim skirt and white camisole as they walked to the row of elevators. Two women in cocktail dresses and expensive jewelry followed them into the elevator. The elevator hummed as it moved, then the door opened at eighteen.

"This is our floor," Storm said.

They walked down the hall and stopped in front of a double door, then Storm slipped in the keycard. When they stepped inside, Melanie's eyes widened. The entrance to the suite had hardwood floors, a high dark wood table with a lamp, and a large bathroom off to the left, then they stepped into a huge living space with a couch and chairs, a bar at the end, and a dining table that would seat eight. To the right was a door that she presumed led to the bedroom.

She gazed at Storm and realized she was totally alone with him in a hotel room. A shiver of anticipation danced down her spine and her heart rate accelerated. He tossed the keycard on the table and turned to her with a smile.

"Finally I have you all to myself." He led her to the living room and took her in his arms for a deep kiss. Then he sat down on the couch, stretching his arm across the back in invitation for her to join him.

Instead, she glanced around at their posh surroundings.

"So in this place, are you Storm, the musician, or Rafe Ranier, billionaire businessman?"

"What would the difference be?" he asked with a smile.

"Well, if you were Rafe Ranier, I might be embarrassed to do this." She grasped the hem of her camisole and raised it, baring her midriff. His eyes lit up as she revealed her naked breasts, then pulled the top all the way off and tossed aside the bit of lace and cotton.

"Storm. I'm definitely Storm," he insisted, staring at her chest.

She laughed and stroked her fingertips over the tattoo on her breast as she sauntered toward him. His intense gaze sent need quivering through her.

"You said you wanted a closer look at my tattoo." She stopped in front of him, her breast at his eye level.

He touched her breast with one calloused fingertip and traced the outline of the bluebird. Heat shimmered through her.

"It's beautiful."

She smiled and stepped out of her sandals, then unfastened her skirt and dropped it to the floor. Now she stood before him in only her skimpy turquoise lace panties. His appreciative gaze sent her confidence soaring, and as much as she wanted to fling herself into his arms, she wanted to revel in it a bit longer. She tucked her hands behind her head and stretched, thrusting her bosom forward. Then she turned and walked away, with a sway to her hips.

"Right back." She sauntered to the bar and opened the fridge, then grabbed a bottle of imported beer. She opened it, then walked toward him again, pressing the cold bottle to her chest. His gaze locked on the bottle nestled between her breasts and she smiled seductively as she glided it across her breast, then over the nipple, which immediately tightened to a hard nub.

She perched on his denim-clad knees, curling one hand around his neck.

"You must be thirsty after your *long, hard* performance

on stage." She wriggled her behind, definitely feeling something long and hard beneath her.

She held the open bottle to his lips and he took it from her and gulped it back. Then his head lowered to her breast.

Shock pulsed through her at the feel of his cool lips surrounding her nipple, then cold, bubbly beer washing against her sensitive nub. He swallowed, then licked her other nipple with his cold tongue. She wrapped both arms around his neck and he kissed her lips, his beer-flavored tongue swirling inside her mouth.

She smiled. "I can't believe a big rock star like you chose me from among all those other women," she said, falling into the role of a groupie. She nuzzled his neck.

"That's right, baby. You were just too sexy to turn down." His hand stroked over her breast, then his thumb rolled over the nipple. Excitement danced through her. "Especially after you flashed these beautiful tits of yours."

"I'm so glad you chose me," she said breathlessly. "This is a fantasy come true." She nuzzled his ear. "It's something I've always dreamed about, but never thought would actually happen."

He smiled, his blue eyes glittering. "Tell me, do you touch yourself when you dream of me?"

She smiled shyly. "Yes . . . but I'd rather touch you."

She slid from his lap and crouched in front of him, watching the heat simmering in his eyes as she slowly unzipped him.

"I'll do anything you want," she said. "I'm here for your pleasure."

He leaned back on the couch, then crossed his hands behind his head. "Why don't you prove it then? Show me what you can do."

She reached inside his boxers and wrapped her hand around the hot steel shaft hidden within. When she drew it out, she almost gasped.

She knew from the previous encounter that he was big, but seeing his cock up close in the light was amazing. It was thick and long, with veins pulsing along the side. Her fingers barely fit around it.

"Am I too big for you? Because if I am, I can arrange for another girl to come in here," he teased.

"Oh no." She met his heated gaze with one of her own. "This is all mine."

She reached for his bottle of beer and took a sip, then with the cold liquid still in her mouth, she stretched her lips around the bulbous tip and took it in her mouth.

"Shit, that feels so—"

But he groaned as she began to suck.

He tangled his fingers in her hair as she glided down his shaft a little. The feel of his big, hard cock in her mouth made her tremble with desire. She clenched her thighs together in need, longing for him to thrust inside her.

Still holding his erection with one hand, she cupped his soft balls in the other and lightly squeezed them, then caressed. His head fell back against the couch, and the sight of the heat blazing from his eyes sent her hormones surging. She leaned down and licked one sac. At his soft moan, a deep sense of satisfaction washed through her, knowing how much she was pleasing him. She drew it into her mouth and teased it with her tongue.

"Oh, yeah, baby." He cupped her head, his tense fingers stretched along her scalp.

His breathing accelerated as she moved her hand up and down his cock, feeling the soft skin glide over the steel shaft beneath. Excitement danced through her as she teased his sac with her tongue, then sucked in light pulses.

His pelvis arched and she could tell he was close.

She drew back, but his fingers flexed and he pressed her to him again.

"Oh, baby, don't stop."

Something about having the powerful man at her mercy spiked her desire higher, and she moaned against his flesh. She took the other ball in her mouth and squeezed the two together, still stroking his cock.

He tensed and she bolted to his cockhead and took it in her mouth a split second before he erupted in a blast of white-hot liquid. She sucked as he pulsed into her, stroking his shaft with her hand.

Finally, he collapsed on the couch.

She tipped her head and smiled at him.

"I think you liked that."

He opened his eyes and growled, then she found herself flipped onto her back on the couch, with him crouching on the floor beside her. He grabbed the beer bottle, which he'd deposited on the side table and held it over her, then tipped it. A dribble of cool amber liquid filled her belly button. He then swooped down and lapped it up. As his tongue continued to pulse into her navel, she felt him glide her panties down, then flick them off. She gazed at him as he kissed her stomach, moving downward. When his cool tongue lapped over her moist folds, she sucked in a breath.

He stared at her pinkness with a grin on his face. He grasped her knees and tucked them over his broad shoulders, then used his thumbs to separate her folds and poured beer onto her. It pooled in her opening and she gasped at the coldness, then again at his hot tongue lapping the liquid and licking her. Then he drove his tongue into her passage, sending heat rushing through her.

He sucked the beer from her, then found her clit and teased it with the tip of his tongue.

"Oh, Storm. Yes." Her fingers curled through his hair as she drew him closer.

He licked and sucked her little button and she gasped as intense pleasure swelled through her. She writhed beneath him, then moaned as a powerful orgasm blasted through her.

She arched and rode the wave, then finally collapsed. When she opened her eyes, she saw that his cock stood fully erect again, and she expected him to prowl over her and glide inside her, but instead, he scooped her up and carried her to the bedroom.

The bed was soft beneath her back. He stepped back and stared at her. She was fully naked and he was still dressed, his cock jutting out of his unzipped jeans. He tugged off his T-shirt and tossed it aside, revealing his sculpted, tattooed chest, then stripped off his pants and boxers in one swift motion.

He walked toward her, magnificent in his nakedness, his muscles rippling.

She could hardly believe this was really happening. She'd wanted to be with Rafe Ranier for so long. That was heaven enough, but this . . . this was Storm, and being with him was beyond anything she'd ever dreamed possible.

Her insides ached at the sight of his long cock bobbing up and down. She wanted it inside her, filling her completely. She wanted him to grind into her, plunging inside until she screamed his name.

But he didn't prowl over her and thrust inside as she expected. He lay down beside her and stroked her hair from her face.

"You are so beautiful."

She smiled. "Do you say that to all your groupies?"

But he didn't laugh. He shook his head. "You are very special, and someone I've wanted to get to know for a long time."

She leaned up on her elbow. "Then why didn't you?"

But she knew why. She'd worked for him.

"I didn't want to ruin our working relationship, but more than that. I guess I didn't feel worthy."

Shock vaulted through her. "What? How could you not be worthy?"

His lips compressed. "You know what my father was like."

She had worked for Rafe when his father was still alive. The man had been stern and authoritative. He had been hard to be around. Very critical and demanding. And totally uncompromising.

"I was never good enough for him. Not me. Not my friends. And no woman I ever dated. Even if we hadn't had the boss-secretary thing between us, I never would have wanted to drag you into a situation like that. He would have wound up driving you away."

"But you dated other women back then."

"Never seriously." He stroked her hair behind her ear. "And I guess I always realized there could be something serious between us. That's why I just decided you were off-limits."

She just stared at his sky blue eyes, glowing with warmth. Could she dare hope it was true?

His lips captured hers in a warm, sweet kiss. Her arms swept around him and she held him close as his tongue curled over hers and undulated in a dance of passion. She arched against him, wanting to feel his body against hers, then reached down and grasped his thick cock and glided it over her thighs. He rolled over her, holding his weight on his elbows as she guided his thick cock between her legs. When it nudged her slick flesh, he pressed forward, stretching her opening as he glided inside. Their gazes locked as he pressed deeper inside her. Then deeper still. Her eyelids flicked closed briefly as pleasure shimmered through her, then she opened them again to meet his gaze.

Once he was fully inside her, he continued to watch her. There was a depth of emotion she couldn't read. Then he drew back and surged deep again, taking her breath away.

He moved in a fluid rhythm, smooth as silk as he

filled her deeply again and again. She clung to his broad shoulders as his cock pumped into her, stoking her desire to a feverish pitch. Her fingernails dug into his flesh as a surge of pleasure rushed through her, then she gasped, and moaned long and loud.

He thrust faster, driving her pleasure higher.

"Oh, God. I'm going to . . ." She sucked in a breath, as bliss seared through her. "Oh, Storm." She tightened her grip on his shoulders. "Yes."

She wailed as he flung her to ecstasy.

He continued to pump into her, then groaned his own release.

Finally, he dropped onto her, then rolled to his side, still holding her close. She could hear his rapidly beating heart. She lay there contentedly, listening to it slow to normal, along with his breathing. Her eyelids fell closed as her excitement turned to a blissful elation, then she dozed off.

Melanie opened her eyes to the bright sunshine. Storm's arm was tossed over his head, and her gaze glided along the tattoos adorning his arms, then across his chest. She still couldn't believe she'd finally lived out her fantasy of being with him.

His eyes opened and he smiled. "Hey, there."

She smiled back. "Hi."

"What were you thinking about so intensely?"

"Oh, just . . ." She shook her head. "It doesn't matter."

"Sure it does. Tell me."

"I was just thinking how lucky I am. Last night was incredible."

He chuckled, a deep rumble in his chest. "Hey, I was pretty lucky, too."

She laughed. "Why? You didn't get to sleep with a hunky, burgeoning rock star last night."

"Maybe not, but I got to be with you." He tugged her to him and kissed her, then rolled her over, their mouths still joined.

She ran her hand over his rock-hard chest, loving the feel of him ravaging her mouth with his tongue, his body pinning her to the bed.

"Is that all you were thinking?" he asked once he released her mouth.

"I've wanted this to happen between us for a long time," she admitted.

"So you're saying you lusted after me when I was your boss?"

"Well, of course. You were the sexiest boss in the world."

"So we both finally got smart and pursued our mutual attraction." His lips brushed hers. "It was worth the wait. I'm glad you picked me for that wild, crazy fling you talked about."

Doubts suddenly flared inside her. Now that they'd crossed the line and ended up in bed together, what came next?

He stroked her hair back from her face. "Melanie, you did realize that I'm not looking for a commitment right now, didn't you? I mean, after the disaster of a relationship I had with Jessica, I'm not ready for more than that right now."

She shook her head. "Oh, of course. I get that."

But her heart sank. She *had* been hoping it was more than a fling. Especially when he'd acted so possessive of her around Travis.

Now that she'd finally experienced what she'd dreamed of for so long, she knew for sure it wasn't a simple crush, or infatuation. She had real feelings for him. If, or rather, when it ended between them, how would she get over him?

Storm drove the bike along the highway heading back to the city, Melanie's arms tight around his waist.

What the hell had he been thinking? He really liked Melanie, and last night had been incredibly intense and sexy, but was he leading her on? Of course, he wanted to keep seeing her . . . and sleeping with her . . . but was that really fair to her? After the disaster of a relationship with Jessica, he wasn't ready to jump into relationship-land again. Even with a woman as fun and delightful as Melanie.

On the other hand, to stop now would make Melanie feel like a discarded one-night stand. And he didn't want to stop. Hopefully, they could continue a casual relationship and still remain friends.

The bell over the door rang as Melanie returned to the back with the bucket and mop she'd used to clean up the cream that had spilled all over the floor when a customer had accidentally knocked over a full jug. There were about six customers in line, but both Sue and Karen, the manager, were on bar, so everything was well in hand.

"Hey, Melanie. There's a hot guy here to see you."

Melanie glanced up at Sue, who'd popped her head in the doorway.

"Storm's here?" She smiled, despite her concern that Karen would be annoyed at her having a friend stop by to see her.

"No, not Storm. This is a new incredibly sexy hunk." Sue grinned. "Man, you've got to tell me where you've been hanging out, because I definitely want to get me one of those."

Melanie washed her hands, then hurried to the front, wondering who it might be.

She glanced around as she stepped through the doorway.

"Hi, Melanie."

She turned toward the vaguely familiar voice and was shocked to see Storm's friend, Travis, stand up from one of the small round tables near the cash register. In his jeans and sleeveless T-shirt, his muscular arms and shoulders were on full display. He looked tough, but very sexy.

Unlike Storm's tattoo-laden arms, Travis had one snake tattoo encircling his bicep. His longish sandy hair was unkempt, in a stylish way, and his strong jaw was shadowed with whiskers.

"Oh, hi. How are you doing?" Why in the world was Travis here?

Storm's words echoed through her head. *Travis and I*

are good friends, but if he could steal you away, he would. It's just
a weird rivalry that started between us when we were on the road.

His smile was boyish and wickedly sexy at the same
time.

"I wanted to know if you'd join me for lunch."

"Well, I'm not sure if—"

"Oh, my God. You're Travis, the lead singer of Savage Kiss." A young woman who'd been sitting with two
friends at a table a few feet away bolted to her feet and
rushed over. "I saw your show last week. You were amazing."

Travis smiled. "Thanks, darlin'."

She thrust a menu at him. "Can I get your autograph?"

"Oh, me, too," one of her friends said. Both young
women had joined her and they were crowding around
him.

He signed autographs for all three of them, and a few
other people who came over.

He turned to Melanie and placed his hand on her
shoulder. "Please say you'll join me and we can go somewhere quiet."

Sue walked over. "Hi, I'm Sue." She grinned broadly
as she held out her hand.

Travis shook it. "Nice to meet you, Sue."

"Travis, that's our supervisor over there. I happen to
know she saw your concert on Thursday night and is a
big fan. I'm sure she'd be thrilled if you go say hi, and I
doubt she'd turn you down if you ask if Melanie can leave
for lunch a little early."

"Thanks for the tip, Sue. I'll be right back."

"What are you doing, Sue?" Melanie said as soon as Travis stepped away. "I'm seeing Storm."

"Listen, Mel, you have two sexy men pursing you." She winked. "Keep your options open."

Travis strolled back to Melanie. "Ready?"

"I . . . guess so."

Melanie and Travis sat down at the table on the patio of Genaro's, a little café a couple of blocks from the shop. The hostess handed them menus, and after a quick glance at the specials, Melanie closed hers.

When the waitress came by, Melanie ordered the chicken-and-pineapple wrap with a salad and Travis asked for a beer and a burger.

"I'm surprised you came to see me," Melanie said.

"Why?"

She couldn't help staring at his blue-green eyes, which sent waves of warmth through her every time he focused on her, which felt like all the time. It was as if she was all he could see.

After years of working with Rafe and feeling invisible, it was a heady feeling. He continued to watch her with unabashed interest, as if he could peer into her soul and know her deepest secrets.

"Well, you don't really know me. And I didn't think you were staying in the city."

"I wanted to spend some time with my sister. I only met her fiancé briefly when they came to see us play on

Thursday, and we didn't get much time to talk. I can't let my little sister just marry some guy without getting to know him."

She smiled. "And do you approve?"

He grinned. "That depends. Do you like the guy?"

"Mr. Ranier? Yes, of course."

"You call him Mr. Ranier?" He shrugged. "I guess he was your boss. Yeah, he seems a bit overbearing to me, but he seems to make Jess happy."

She nodded.

"And as for not knowing you," he smiled, "I wouldn't mind changing that."

"Is that why you asked me to lunch?" She pushed a loose strand of hair, which had escaped the elastic that bound it, behind her ear. "You know I'm seeing Storm."

He shrugged. "I asked you here because I want to get an engagement gift for Jess and I want it to be something special. I thought I could ask your advice. Maybe you'd even help me pick it out."

"Oh, that's nice of you." She nodded. "Sure, I could do that."

The waitress brought their food and she picked up her fork. As she enjoyed a bite of her salad, she gazed at Travis.

Just being at the same table with him set her off balance. Despite his tough-guy attire, he had a sensual aura about him, and she sensed the soul of an artist in him. She felt a strange desire to run her fingers through his sandy brown hair. As if reading her mind, he pushed a lock behind his ear, revealing three small hoop earrings.

Why couldn't she stop thinking about how sexy he was? Was she forming an addiction to rock musicians? Or with Travis, was the appeal that when he looked at her, he seemed to truly see her?

He glanced up and caught her staring at him. A slow smile spread across his face.

"So, darlin', just how serious are you and Storm?"

The limo pulled up outside the coffee shop where Melanie worked and Rafe got out. He'd tried texting her about twenty minutes ago to ask her to lunch, but she hadn't responded yet, so he figured he'd stop by and ask her in person. She didn't keep her cell with her while she was working, so that meant she probably hadn't left for lunch yet.

He stepped into the shop and saw the smiling Sue serving a customer, and another woman he didn't recognize wiping a table by the window.

"Oh, hi," Sue said when she saw him. "Um . . . Melanie's not here right now."

"That's too bad. I was going to take her to lunch."

"I'll let her know you stopped by."

"Excuse me."

Rafe turned to the other woman who now stood beside Sue behind the counter.

He smiled. "Yes?"

She examined his face. "Aren't you in Savage Kiss, too?"

Too?

"Yes, I am."

Her eyes lit up the same way he'd seen a thousand times before when a female fan recognized him, which boosted his ego every time. But right now he wanted to know who else she'd seen from the band, and when.

"I thought so. You're Storm, the guitarist." She smiled brightly. "You're all really good, but you're my favorite."

"Thank you very much."

If he had been wearing his jeans, he'd have smiled wickedly and called her baby, since the fans loved that so much, but in his suit it just felt . . . odd being recognized. No one had ever recognized him as Storm when he was in his suit before. Actually, no one in Philadelphia had ever recognized Storm from Savage Kiss. The band was becoming well-known now, so if he continued to play with them when they were in town, it would start to happen more often. That could become disruptive.

"Have any of the other band members come in?" he asked.

"Yes, the lead singer, Travis, came in about an hour ago. He took Melanie to lunch."

Somehow, Rafe maintained his calm smile without even a flinch.

"Do you know where he took her?"

He noticed Sue glance nervously at the other woman.

"There's a nice café on the corner two blocks east of here called Genaro's. The staff often go there for meals. The other likely place is Freida's Diner another block farther."

"Thanks." He turned and headed to the door.

Why had Travis taken Melanie to lunch? He fumed. As if he didn't know. Fuck, he needed to tell Travis to lay off. That this woman was off-limits. But knowing Travis, that would only make him pursue her harder.

Why the hell would Melanie agree to go with Travis after he'd told her Travis would steal her away in a minute? Of course, despite the incredible night of sex they'd shared, there was no promise of anything more. Certainly nothing that said they were exclusive.

Once on the street, he started east, but his limo pulled up to the curb. The driver got out of the car to open the door.

Melanie shifted in her chair as Travis stared at her with those unnerving blue-green eyes of his, waiting for her answer as to whether she was serious about Storm or not.

"You're hesitating." He reached forward and took her hand, then stroked her wrist. "That makes me think maybe I do have a shot with you."

He raised her hand to his mouth and kissed her palm, sending tremors through her.

She knew she should pull her hand away, but she was mesmerized by his touch.

"Hell, no!"

Her head jerked around as she saw Rafe barreling into the restaurant, his nostrils flaring.

Rock Hard

Melanie sucked in a breath as Travis glanced around at Rafe marching toward the table. Travis winked at Melanie, then turned back to Rafe again.

"Hey, man. What's with the suit?"

"Screw that. Keep your hands off Melanie." Rafe now stood beside Travis, glowering down at him.

Travis shrugged. "I don't see Melanie complaining."

Rafe grabbed a handful of Travis's shirt and dragged him to his feet, then glared him straight in the eye. "I said . . . Don't. Touch. Melanie." He spoke with clenched teeth, sparks flaring from his eyes.

Melanie was aghast. She'd never seen Rafe behave this way.

A waiter hovered in the background, looking uncertain, and the other diners sent nervous glances their way.

She pushed herself to her feet. "I'm not going to sit here while the two of you act like children." Then she strode from the restaurant without a backward glance. In her peripheral vision, she saw Rafe release Travis's shirt, but as she walked along the sidewalk away from the patio, she heard angry male voices. Then she turned the corner and they were lost in the noise of the traffic and passersby.

It thrilled her that Rafe was so possessive of her. But it also made her angry.

Storming into the restaurant as if he owned her. Whatever they had between them was tentative at best. He had admitted that he didn't want a relationship right now, so he had no right to scare men away from her.

The next morning, Rafe raked his fingers through his hair, the newspaper laid out in front of him on his desk. Just his luck that someone had taken pictures of his confrontation with Travis on their cell phone.

"I thought you could use this." Jessica walked in the open door of his office with a steaming cup of coffee in her hand. She set it down beside the paper and smiled. "Really? Fisticuffs?"

He sipped the hot coffee as he stared at the picture of him slugging Travis in the face. "Who says fisticuffs?"

She laughed. "Okay. Murderous rampage then."

"Jess, if I were in the mood for jokes, I'd laugh, but right now . . ." He sat back in his chair and groaned.

She leaned against his desk. "Look, I think it's sweet that you got jealous and punched my brother out. Having grown up with him, there were many times I wanted to do the same thing."

He glanced at her in surprise. "You're not mad?"

"No." She smiled. "But I do think it says you have

feelings for Melanie." She rested her hand on her chest. "Which I think is sweet. Especially since I know she's sweet on you. Have you told her how you feel?"

He shrugged. "I don't know how I feel." Jessica should know more than most. He'd believed he was totally in love with her, and she had felt the same about him, but in the end they both realized it was Dane she was meant to be with.

She pointed at the paper. "Really? You're sticking with that?"

He scowled and pushed the paper aside. "Damn, what a shitstorm."

The headline read, SAVAGE, BUT NO KISS, then the article talked about how Rafe Ranier, head of the huge conglomerate Ranier Industries, confronted lead singer of the band Savage Kiss. It went on to reveal the fact that Rafe was also Storm, popular guitarist with the band, though they didn't have all the facts straight.

"I hear Dane isn't too thrilled with you. He's set up a few meetings with key business partners to discuss the article and ensure they aren't uncomfortable with a rock musician being one of the executives at Ranier Industries."

"Great, so I've disappointed my brother, punched your brother—"

"And given him some great press."

"None of that matters." Rafe rubbed his hands over his face. "Not when I've disappointed Melanie. She stormed out of the restaurant and I doubt she'll even talk to me again."

"She might be annoyed," Jessica said, "but I'm sure she'll talk to you again. Especially if you tell her how you feel."

At a knock on her apartment door, Melanie put down her magazine and walked across the room. She peered through the peephole to see Storm standing on the other side of the door. Her heart leapt at the sight of him, but lingering annoyance still remained.

She pulled open the door. "Hello."

"Hi," he said with a sheepish smile, then held up a bouquet of flowers. White roses and a stem of pink lady slipper orchids.

She took the flowers and breathed in the delicate scent of the roses. "They're lovely. Thanks."

"May I come in?"

She nodded and stepped back. He came in and closed the door.

"I'll go put these in water."

Storm followed her into the kitchen, where he watched as she grabbed a vase from the cupboard over the sink and filled it with water, then cut the ends off the stems before she put the flowers into the vase.

"Melanie, I want to apologize for yesterday."

"Apologize for what exactly?" It was great that he wanted to make amends, but was he just apologizing in general, or did he understand what he'd done wrong?

"Trick question, right?" He gazed at her, as if seeking a clue to what she was looking for. "I'm sorry I interrupted your lunch with Travis, and that I started a confrontation with him. And I'm sorry I hit him."

Surprise rocked through her. "You hit him?"

"I take it you haven't seen the newspaper today."

"It was in the paper?"

Storm sighed. "Yeah. It seems someone took pictures on their cell phone. I guess it was a slow news day."

"Or they thought their audience would be interested in an executive from a huge company getting in a fight with a rock musician. I bet your brother isn't too happy with you."

"True."

"Oh, I guess Jessica isn't either, since it was her brother you hit."

He shrugged. "She seemed to think he probably deserved it."

Melanie laughed despite herself. "Is Travis okay?"

"Yeah. I didn't mark that pretty face of his."

"That's good."

At Storm's sharp sidelong glance, she could tell his jealousy was as strong as ever.

"So back to your apology, which wasn't sufficient."

"Why not?"

At her frown, he said, "Huh." Then he scratched his head. "Uh . . . could you help me out here?"

Damn. Men never got it.

"You want to apologize for not trusting me."

He leaned back against the counter. "That's the whole thing, isn't it? It's not just that I didn't trust you. It's that there was no reason for you not to take Travis up on whatever proposition he made, because . . ." He shrugged. "I told you I wasn't ready for a relationship right now. And that meant we had no commitment."

He pushed away from the counter and stepped toward her. Maybe he wasn't so clueless after all.

He stood in front of her and stroked back a strand of hair behind her ear. Her skin tingled at the gentle caress.

"I was a fool." He cupped her cheek. "And I don't want to lose you."

She watched, mesmerized, as his face approached hers. His lips brushed hers, lightly at first, then more firmly as he drew her close to his body. She wrapped her arms around his neck and melted against him, his kiss igniting her inner need.

When he drew back, his sky blue eyes questioning, she smiled.

"So, Mr. Ranier, are you asking me to go steady?"

He grinned. "That's exactly what I'm asking."

Melanie finished putting on her mascara and gazed critically at her face in the mirror. The dark kohl around her eyes, along with the muted earth-tone shadows, made her green eyes look bigger, and the blush gave her pale cheeks a soft flush of color.

She glanced at the clock. It was time to go.

As much as Melanie had wanted to fall into bed with Storm after his apology last night, she'd had plans with friends she couldn't change, so he'd promised they'd do something special tonight. He'd offered to take her to a fancy restaurant with dancing and maybe a show, but she'd told him she would rather be with him somewhere they could be alone. He'd smiled and suggested dinner and a movie at his place.

She ran a brush through her long, dark blonde hair,

then walked through the living room, stopping to take a sniff of the lovely roses before grabbing her sweater from the front closet and heading out the door toward the elevator. Moments later, as soon as she pushed open the lobby door, she saw the black limo waiting for her. She stepped outside into the warm evening air.

"Melanie, hi. I was coming up to get you." Storm stood a few paces ahead on the sidewalk. He walked alongside her the few steps to the car and the chauffeur opened the back door.

Storm followed her into the limo and settled in the seat beside her. He wore his jeans this evening, but with a black button-up shirt rather than a T-shirt or tank top like she'd usually seen him in as Storm. It was a nice compromise between Storm, the rock guitarist and Rafe, the businessman.

Of course, no matter how he was dressed, he still revved her engine. She could lean into his arms right now and ravage those full, sexy lips of his.

He glanced toward her and smiled. "What are you thinking about?" His eyes glittered. "Me, I hope."

She stroked her finger along the placket of his shirt, from the neck to the second button, which was open, revealing a hint of the tattoos on his chest.

"I'm looking forward to getting to your place."

He nuzzled her cheek. "If you were to keep looking at me like that and we had more than just another two blocks to go, I'd say we wouldn't make it to my place."

She laughed and turned her face up, then brushed her lips against his. His arms went around her and she melted against his solid chest as she explored his mouth.

Then the car slowed down and pulled up in front of a tall building. As the chauffeur got out of the car, Storm eased away, then the back door opened and she climbed out of the car. She walked with Storm toward the glass doors of the building in front of them. A doorman opened the door for them and they stepped into the air-conditioned lobby. It was lovely, with cream marble floors and walls, a sitting area of leather couches and tables, and lots of huge floral arrangements. The ceilings were off-white with crossed beams, and a section of the wall was covered in stacked slate, contrasting nicely with the shiny marble.

As his secretary, Melanie had arranged for the care of Rafe's apartment when he was gone, everything from having the place cleaned regularly to someone watering the plants, but she'd never been here. They stepped into the elevator, and Storm pushed the top button, then entered a code on a keypad beside it.

"Your apartment building is beautiful."

He shrugged. "I like it."

He slid his arm around her and she smiled as the floor numbers flickered by. The elevator doors opened onto a bright, spacious penthouse apartment. The dark hardwood floors of the entryway gleamed in the light from the setting sun cascading in from the huge windows. In the living room, bright accent cushions in red, orange, and yellow added a nice contrast to the beige leather and dark wood furniture. The bright colors were carried through the artwork and flowering plants, adding a warmth and flair to the space.

"I didn't realize it would be this huge." She pulled off

her shoes, then walked across the decadently plush carpet to stare out the window at the stunning view of the city cascaded in the golden light of the sunset.

He gestured to the couch facing a big fireplace. "Sit down and I'll get you a drink. Champagne?"

Her gaze flicked to his. "Really? Are we celebrating something?"

He smiled. "Just being with you."

He took a bottle from an ice bucket on a stand and popped the cork without waiting for her response, then he poured the bubbly liquid into a delicate flute and handed it to her.

She sipped, the tingly bubbles tickling her nose.

Her eyes widened. *So this is what nirvana tastes like.*

Clearly, she'd never had really *good* quality champagne before. As wonderful as this was, drinking fantastic champagne while sitting in this luxurious penthouse, having ridden here in a chauffeur-driven limo, it left her feeling unsettled. Rafe was totally used to this lifestyle. He'd never had to worry about money, and even though he'd spent a year living out of a backpack, he knew he had money if he ever needed it. Not like her. She had to worry about bringing in enough money to make the next month's rent.

As fun as it was being with Rafe, it was startlingly clear that they came from entirely different worlds.

"What are you thinking about?" Storm asked.

She smiled. "Oh, nothing important."

Her phone buzzed and she pulled it from her pocket to check the incoming text.

"It's from my mom. She wants to know if I can make it home for Dad's birthday next month."

"That's nice. Are you going?"

She shrugged. "I don't know yet. I don't know if I can justify the cost of the trip."

"You're really on a tighter budget with the new job I take it."

She shrugged. "A little." Actually, a lot, but then freedom had its cost.

"What does your mother think of you working as a barista?"

"Are you kidding? She'd freak out if she knew I'd quit my job at your firm. She was so proud of me for being an executive assistant at a big company, with a stable job, regular hours, and with benefits."

He smiled. "With benefits?"

She laughed at the sexy grin on his face.

"Yes, well, not the kind of benefits you're thinking of."

"It's too bad we didn't allow ourselves to explore a relationship back then," he said.

She grinned. "Really? You would have wanted that?" She sat forward, then swiveled around onto his lap, her knees hugging his thighs, then flattened her hand on his chest. "Me coming into your office and you knowing you couldn't touch me." Her hand slid slowly down his solid chest. She could feel the ridges of his hard muscles beneath the cotton of his shirt.

"Wait, that sounds like what we did have."

"You wouldn't really have expected me to have sex with you in the office, would you?" Her hand slid to her own chest and lightly glided over her breast. "You'd just have to bear having me close, knowing what's under my conservative white blouse."

She cupped her breast and caressed it. Heat flared in his blue eyes. She leaned back a little and stroked down her belly with the other hand.

"And what's under my linen skirt." Her fingers glided over the crotch of her jeans. "Knowing I was hot and longing for you, too, but not doing anything about it."

She was surprised he wasn't drooling as he watched her hand caress the denim. Her fingertip strokes were so light she couldn't feel it through the thick fabric, but her nipples were hard as beads and her insides ached.

She slid her hand to his thigh, then up. "I bet you would get hard as rock under your expensive, designer business suit." A tremor rippled through her at the feel of the huge bulge under the denim. She squeezed, eliciting a groan, then wrapped her fingers around it as best she could and rubbed up and down.

She leaned in close and murmured in his ear, "Then there we'd be, both frustrated and horny."

He drew in a deep breath. "And we wouldn't do anything about it?" he asked doubtfully.

"No." She drew her hand from his shaft and pressed her body down on him. Then she pivoted forward, gliding her crotch along his hard bulge.

Oh God, that feels good.

She pivoted again and again. His hardness stroking against her, stoking her desire. She wrapped her hands around his shoulders for purchase. His hands gripped her hips and he directed her rocking motion, speeding her up. She had found her rhythm now, electric sensations shimmering through her. One of his hands glided forward, then released the button of her jeans, then drew the zipper down. His fingers slipped inside and found her warmth. Heat flushed through her as he located her clit, then teased it as she glided over him.

Oh, God.

Her fingers clamped around him as she felt a tide of pleasure rising in her. She wanted to ride it all the way, but she also wanted to savor the moment.

After a few seconds, she drew in a deep breath, then pulled away from Rafe, eliciting a groan of frustration. She smiled wickedly. "See? Would you really have wanted this kind of frustration?"

A wicked smile curved his lips. "Well, maybe I would have demanded something different."

She raised an eyebrow. "Really?" She smiled. "Well, we'll never know now."

She stood up and turned around, but he hooked a finger under a belt loop of her jeans, preventing her from moving forward. She laughed as she turned around to face him.

"That's unacceptable," Rafe said. "Since I'm the boss, I think I should have some say in this."

She tipped her head. "And exactly what do you want to say?"

"Well, first of all, I think you should show proper respect and call me Mr. Ranier."

Excitement quivered through her. "But you always told me to call you Rafe."

Damn, why had she said that? This was role-playing. But the words had slipped out automatically, probably because she'd always felt odd calling him by his first name while calling his brother Mr. Ranier.

"Right now, in *this* office, I want you to call me Mr. Ranier." He tugged on the belt loop of her jeans, pulling them down a little. "You know, jeans are totally inappropriate in the office." He sent her a glance full of steel. "Take them off."

Quivers danced down her spine. She pushed the jeans down to her ankles, then stepped out of them. It was so odd that even though he was wearing jeans and she thought of him as Storm, as soon as they fell into the role of boss and secretary, he immediately became Rafe again. Though not the Rafe she had known. He was a Rafe she had only dreamed about. A Rafe who demanded she call him Mr. Ranier, and who would order her to do unspeakable, sexy things.

He nodded. "You can't sit around the office in your panties. Take those off, too."

She hooked her fingers under the elastic of her pretty pink panties and glided them slowly down her legs then over her feet and held them up. He took them from her hand and slid them into his jeans pocket.

"Now sit."

She sat down beside him on the couch, the leather

cool against her intimate parts. He stood up and dropped his pants and boxers to the floor, then sat down again, his fully erect cock jutting up between his legs.

"Pull up your shirt so I can see your breasts."

She grabbed the hem and drew it up, revealing her feminine, pink lace bra. She started to pull the top over her head, but he stopped her.

"I said pull it up, not take it off." The cold edge to his voice made her hands tremble with desire.

She released the fabric, leaving it bunched above her breasts. He reached forward and stroked over her lace cups, then his hands covered her and he gently pulsed around her, sending heat pumping through her.

"They're lovely." He smiled. "And I see this bra is front-opening." He reached for the clasp and squeezed. The pressure of the elastic around her torso released. He drew the cups away, revealing her naked breasts, the nipples pointing straight forward.

He stroked over one hard nub with his fingertip and she moaned.

"Now you touch them."

She stroked her fingertip over one bead-like nipple. Heat thrummed through her. She touched the other, then pinched them both between her fingertips.

"Does that feel good?" he asked.

"Not as good as when you touch them."

He chuckled. "Now I want you to touch your pussy."

She glided one had down her stomach, then over her mound, feeling a little self-conscious as he watched her intently. She stroked over her slick flesh, still sensitive from the hard rubbing of the denim. She swirled inside.

"Touch your clit."

She found the little button in the nest of flesh and quivered over it. Her breathing increased as hot sensations pulsed through her.

"Show me how you make yourself come, Melanie." His words, heavy and full of need, spurred her on.

"Yes, Mr. Ranier," she said as she flicked her clit, then quivered her fingertip over it.

His burning gaze locked on her fingers as she teased her button. Although his expression was hard and commanding, she could tell by his impossibly rigid erection that he was as turned on as she was.

Still lying on the couch, she arched her pelvis up, giving him a full view of her most intimate parts. "Do you like this, Mr. Ranier?" she said in puffy breaths.

He nodded.

"Because I'm"—she gasped and arched as the intense sensations spiked—"oh . . . I'm so close."

Her body trembled and she gazed at his compelling blue eyes as she felt the heat wash through her.

"Shit." Rafe moved in front of her and as pleasure erupted through her, she felt hot, hard flesh against her. He surged forward, his now rock-hard cock impaling her. She groaned at the hot invasion, then wailed as his pumping drove her pleasure higher.

She wrapped her arms around his big muscular body. "Oh, yes, Mr. Ranier. Oh, please, fuck me hard."

He drove deeper still, then pumped faster. Then he jerked forward and groaned, holding her tight to his body as he erupted inside her.

She sprawled back and he collapsed on her, the weight of his body crushing her into the cushions. They lay there panting for a few moments before he finally pushed himself back, taking his weight on his knees again.

She sent him a glowing smile, then cupped his cheeks and kissed him. "Oh, Mr. Ranier."

He rocked his pelvis forward, and she automatically squeezed around the cock still buried inside her.

"I think in this intimate situation, you should call me Rafe. Or Storm."

She clutched his shirt and pulled him forward for another kiss. "I like calling you Mr. Ranier." She nuzzled his neck. "I like it when you take control." She nipped his ear, but then he drew away, his cock sliding from her body.

"Do you want to take a shower while I get dinner ready?"

She could sense his withdrawal and she wasn't sure why. "I'd rather we take a shower together. Then I could help you with dinner."

As enticement, she glided her fingertips over her breast, then toyed with the soft nipple. Although they were both spent, his eyes glittered and he smiled.

"Deal."

Melanie sat with Sue at the diner, having breakfast before they started their shift. Melanie took a bite of her toast, smeared with strawberry jam.

"So which of your handsome hunks did you go out with this week?" Sue asked.

"I told you, I'm only going out with Storm."

"But Travis is so sexy. Well, so is Storm, but I don't see why you don't date both. After all, you're not exclusive to Storm."

"Well, actually . . ."

Sue's eyes lit up. "Really? That's great."

"I thought you wanted me to play the field."

"Hey, a bird in the hand . . ." Sue shrugged. "I'm just sayin'."

Melanie's cell phone buzzed and she pulled it from her purse and glanced at the text.

"It's a reminder that I have my three-month evaluation next week." She pursed her lips. "I'm a bit worried about it. You know Karen doesn't really like me."

"I don't think it's that she doesn't like you, but I know what you mean. She resents that the previous manager hired you, then was promoted. I think Karen wanted them to hire someone she knows. But she can't fire you just because she doesn't like you."

Melanie glanced at her watch. "No, but she could fire me for being late, so we'd better get going."

Sue took a quick sip of her coffee. "Okay, let's go." She stood up and dropped some bills on the table. It was her turn to pay today.

They stepped outside and walked along the street toward the coffee shop.

"So have you signed up for those art courses you were thinking about?" Sue asked.

"No. I don't want to change my availability with Karen. Booking an evening off every week might annoy her."

"You're allowed to have a life, you know."

"Yeah, I know, but until my evaluation period is over, I'm going to do whatever I can not to rock the boat." She shrugged. "Anyway, I'm not sure I can really afford the lessons right now."

"I could loan you the money."

Melanie smiled. "Thanks, that's sweet, but I'll just wait a bit." She pursed her lips. "I'm actually thinking that maybe I might get a second job. I heard that the specialty makeup shop around the corner is looking for people."

She frequented the shop, watching for the latest polishes and nail-art kits. It might be fun to work there. On the other hand, that would leave her even less time to do her own thing.

Melanie was actually feeling a little depressed about the whole situation. She'd made this career move hoping to open up her options, but instead she felt more hemmed in. If she'd still worked for Rafe, she'd automatically have her evenings free, and she'd have the money to pay for it, so taking the course wouldn't be an issue.

She stared at her bare nails. And she'd be able to wear her beloved nail polish more often. She found herself doing manis less often these days because she had to remove them every time she went to work. Even wearing subdued manicures was better than not wearing nail polish at all.

That didn't mean she wanted to go back to the corporate world, though.

She'd figure it out. On the whole, life was good.

After all, she was sleeping with her dream man.

Melanie handed a coffee to a young woman in a floral sundress as Travis walked in the door.

Sue nudged her elbow. "I thought you said you weren't playing the field. Why's gorgeous rock guy here?"

"He's my friend's brother and I'm going with him to pick out a gift for her engagement."

Sue grinned. "Yeah, well . . ." She winked. "Have fun."

"Hey, there, gorgeous," Travis said when he reached the counter. "Ready to go?"

She glanced at her watch. Ten to four.

"I'll be a few more minutes. Want a latte?"

"Sure."

She made him a latte, then finished up with two more customers before she headed to the back to change. Fifteen minutes later, she accompanied him out the door. They went to a variety of stores, shopping aimlessly at first, but then they passed the window of a little boutique where Melanie spotted a quilt that looked very similar to one Jessica had shown her in a magazine recently. Jessica had said the pattern was called Card Trick and it was like one her grandmother had made and kept on the bed in the guestroom Jessica used to sleep in when she visited her.

"I remember the quilt she's talking about," Travis

said. "It does look a lot like it." He smiled. "She'll love it. She always loved her visits to Gran's."

They went inside and he bought the quilt.

"You'll join me for dinner, right?" he asked.

"Oh, I don't think so."

"But I want to thank you for today." Then he smiled his crooked smile. "Come on. You aren't going to make me eat alone, are you?"

For some reason, she just couldn't resist his boyish, yet incredibly sexy, charm. She knew she was hesitating because Storm wouldn't want her spending time with Travis—even the shopping trip—but she couldn't let Storm's misguided jealousy control her.

She smiled. "Okay."

In the restaurant, they talked over drinks while they waited for their meals to arrive.

"So how's the job going?" Travis asked.

She shrugged. "It's okay. Better than working in an office."

"But not all you'd hoped for?"

"I thought there'd be more time for other things. And my boss doesn't really like me."

"Really? I find that hard to believe."

Melanie sipped her drink. "I was hired just before she was promoted to manager, and I think she'd recommended one of her friends for the job."

"What about your art?" he asked.

"I'm working on it. I've joined an artist community online, and I've posted some things to get more exposure, but I don't really know how I'd turn any of that into income yet."

"What kinds of things do you like to draw? Besides tattoos, that is."

"Oh, all kinds of things, but I really like to draw manga-style art, especially fantasy creatures."

"Have you thought about becoming an illustrator?"

"Oh, sure, I'd love that, but I think it's a tough business to break into. I've been to anime conventions where artists do commissions and make money that way, but I'm not sure it's enough to live on. Whatever I do, I have to practice a lot to get better, and it's so hard to find the time."

"I know what you mean. It was like that for me when the band was just starting out. I had to find time to practice and play gigs while working a full-time job. We tried to book a tour a while ago and a lot of the bigger musical venues turned us away. Now those same managers are begging us to perform there. Just don't give up, and keep working on your art. That's what we did and look how well it's turned out."

She smiled. "I've got to say, it would be exciting to travel around to different cities like you're doing. I'd love to do that. I've always pretty much stayed in one place. Maybe if there were enough big conventions going on around the country, I could go on a sort of tour and get enough commissions to make a living." She smiled wistfully. "But that's just wishful thinking."

He smiled. "Well, if you like the idea of traveling,

you could always come with us. The band is continuing on tour next week and we could use another roadie. You'd get to travel around the country, and you'd have your expenses covered and get paid."

"Oh. I . . . don't think that would work out."

"You haven't even given the idea a chance." He sipped his beer. "And think of all the great experiences you'd have."

Her fingers wrapped around her glass. "I'd have to leave my job."

"Which I get the impression you're not that attached to. And we probably pay more."

She pursed her lips. "And this relationship with Storm is so new. I wouldn't want to put it in jeopardy."

Travis rested his arms on the table and leaned forward. "If it's meant to be, then a little time away won't hurt. And if Storm really cares about you, then he'd want you to be happy. And if going on tour with us makes you happy . . ." He shrugged. "Then he shouldn't have a problem with it."

It was a fantastic opportunity, and she had to admit, she was more than a little tempted.

"Storm would not be happy with me traveling with you."

Travis chuckled. "Yeah, he does tend to get jealous." His gaze locked with hers. "So is it more important that you do what makes Storm happy, or what makes you happy?"

"That's not a simple question. Being with Storm makes me happy."

Travis shrugged. "There's nothing stopping Storm from joining us on tour, too. We never wanted him to leave the band."

Her eyes narrowed. "You're not asking me to put pressure on Storm to rejoin Savage Kiss, are you?"

He took her hand and raised it to his mouth, then brushed it lightly with his lips. "Don't you think I'd be more interested in attracting you?"

She glanced around, almost expecting Storm to appear from nowhere just like the last time she'd been with Travis.

"Even if I did go with you, I'd still be in a relationship with Storm."

He released her hand, his smile never wavering. "I know."

But the twinkle in his eye did not inspire confidence in her that he'd respect that relationship.

"Just think about it," he said.

The next day, Storm picked her up from work on his motorcycle, and they sped back to his place to spend the evening together.

As she clung to his waist, her head resting against his big back, her thoughts turned to the conversation with Travis. Once the waitress had brought their food, they'd changed the topic to the upcoming wedding, which was still several months away, and then on to other small talk.

She really couldn't tell if she was a pawn in a scheme for Travis to attract Storm back to the group, or whether Travis had designs on her. There was definitely a strong attraction between them. Or maybe he really was just being a nice guy and wanted to help her on her quest.

Of course, there was no reason he couldn't be both a nice guy, and hopeful that once away from Storm, she would fall into his arms.

They arrived at Storm's building and he pulled into the underground parking area. Inside the lot, he pulled into the corner, then used a remote to open a garage door to a private storage location where he pulled in with the bike. He dismounted and took off his helmet. She handed him hers, hopped off the bike, and followed him from the small space, then he closed the door.

"So what are you thinking about so hard?" Storm asked.

She gazed up at him as they walked toward the door leading to the elevators.

Some people passed by, so she waited until they entered the elevator and the doors closed.

"I was just thinking about you and the band. Don't you want to go with them when they continue their tour?"

His eyebrows arched. "Are you trying to get rid of me?"

"No, of course not. It's just that you come to life when you play with them, and you're so talented. It seems like a waste."

His gaze flicked to hers and she saw the turmoil in his eyes.

"I've already spent a year away. Now I need to show Dane that he can depend on me. That I'm willing to build the company right alongside him."

"Is it more important to do what makes you happy, or what makes your brother happy?" It was sage advice when Travis had said it to her, and it applied to Storm, too.

His gaze sharpened. "It's not that simple. As I said, I already spent a year away indulging in my own pursuits, while Dane worked to keep the company thriving."

"But he likes doing that. But you . . . that's not where your heart is."

The elevator arrived at his floor and they stepped off into his stunning penthouse apartment. Everything about this place—the expensive furnishings, the spectacular view through the huge windows, the high ceilings, and the sheer size—reminded her that she and Storm came from two very different worlds.

"I thought you'd understand this," he said. "It's about family. About building a relationship with my brother. My family life was never great, but now I have a chance at a real relationship with my brother, without the destructive influence of our father interfering. When we were younger, he used to praise everything Dane did and beat the hell out of me for every little infraction. It made me pull away from Dane, too, and I'm only now realizing my brother was just as much a prisoner as I was."

She nodded. "I know. I get it." It was true. Storm needed to be here. At least for a while. Dane had worked hard to incorporate Rafe's ideas into the company, making it greener and more employee friendly. That had made Rafe very happy, and he wanted to continue to build Ranier Industries into a company he could be proud of, not just because it was his family's legacy, but because it made the world a better place.

"What prompted this discussion?" he asked.

She stared at her fingers. "I talked to Travis yesterday."

Fire blazed in his eyes. "What did he want?"

She pushed back her shoulders. "Actually, we went out shopping together." When his jaw clenched, she continued quickly. "When he took me to lunch that first time," she gazed at Storm, "when you confronted him . . . he had only asked me to join him because he wanted to talk to me about Jessica. He asked me to help him pick out a gift for her."

"That's not the *only* reason he asked you to lunch."

Ignoring his comment, she continued. "That's why we went shopping together yesterday. And . . . we got talking."

Storm's eyes narrowed and she knew it was not a good time to mention Travis' offer. If ever.

"It's just . . . he said they'd love to have you back in the band, and going on tour with them."

"So they're trying to get to me through you?"

She planted her hands on her hips. "Make up your mind. Would you rather Travis be pursuing you or me?"

Surprisingly, Storm chuckled. "Actually, he's not my type." He stepped toward her and slid his arms around her waist, then drew her close. "I'd rather be pursued by you." His lips brushed hers. "And caught."

She laughed. "Actually, I think it might be pretty hot if Travis caught you. Man-on-man action. Yummy!"

His eyes widened and he stroked her shoulders. "Well, aren't you the little pervert?"

"Really? And you'd say no to watching me with another woman? Why do you think women don't have the same fantasy about watching two hot guys together?" She grinned. "Or more?"

She slid her hands up her torso and cupped her breasts. "In fact, just the thought of you and Travis, naked and touching each other's hot hard bodies . . ." She giggled. "I'm getting hot just thinking about it."

In fact, she was quivering with need. She stroked her nipples until they were so hard they practically burst through her shirt, Storm's gaze locked on them.

"And I'm getting fucking hot just watching you."

She grinned as she pulled off her top.

She'd started to regret bringing up her conversation with Travis, and had been worried about how to turn things around so they could enjoy their evening together, but she shouldn't have.

Men were just so easy.

On Monday morning, Melanie decided to pay Rafe a visit at his office. He came to visit her frequently, and she wanted to turn the tables. In fact, she had a surprise for him.

It was odd entering the big lobby of the office building again. She hadn't been here in almost three months. Her high heels clacked against the marble floor as she walked to the elevator. When she got off the elevator on the executive floor, she glanced around at the reception area and she realized she missed it. Not enough to want to return to work here, but there were a lot of good memories in this office.

Mostly ones with Rafe, but also with Jessica once she'd begun to work here. Melanie walked to her old desk, which was empty at the moment.

"Hey, stranger, what are you doing here?"

Melanie glanced up at Jessica's voice. Jessica stood in her teal business suit and white blouse, holding an armful of folders.

"I thought I'd say hi to Rafe."

"Oh, sure. Go ahead in. You don't have too long, though. He has a meeting with the marketing department in fifteen minutes."

"Okay, thanks." That didn't give her much time.

As Melanie walked toward his office, she saw the door was open. Rafe glanced up from his computer screen as she walked in, then smiled.

"Melanie. This is a nice surprise. Come in and sit down. I'll just finish this e-mail." He glanced back at his computer and tapped at the keyboard.

She closed the door behind her and locked it discreetly.

He finished typing and glanced up, pushing his chair back. She walked toward him, and his gaze flickered to her upswept hair, then down her smart, tailored blazer to her short skirt.

"Are you going to a job interview?" he asked.

She shook her head, continuing toward him. "I'm

here," she said in a deep, seductive tone, "to beg for my job back."

Rafe watched her as she continued around his desk toward his chair. Startled, his gaze flicked to hers, but the glitter in her eyes told him this was a role.

"Well, I don't know. Why would I consider hiring you back?" he asked, turning stone-faced.

She took his hand and pulled something from her pocket, then placed a scrap of lace in his palm. He glanced down and realized they were panties.

Her panties.

God, she was naked under that short skirt. His cock twitched.

"Because I will do anything you want," she murmured, her voice dripping with sexual innuendo.

She leaned back against his desk, her thigh pressing against his knee and she tugged the panties from his hand and tucked them into his breast pocket. Then she drew his hand to the hem of her skirt and guided it underneath. At the feel of her warm, naked thigh—God, no pantyhose—his cock twitched again. Then she pressed his fingers against her folds and—fuck, she was soaking wet.

She released his hand and he stroked her slick flesh. She shifted around, then pushed on the armrest of his chair to turn him toward her. His fingers slipped from her slickness as she knelt in front of him, then stroked over the hard bulge in his pants.

"I think I know what you'd like right now." She smiled, and slowly drew down the zipper, then unfastened the button.

Her delicate fingers stroked over the light cotton that covered his hot, aching flesh. Then she reached inside. He sucked in a breath as her fingers wrapped around him. She drew him out, then gazed at his long, hard cock with wide eyes.

"Why, Mr. Ranier, you are so big."

As she stroked him, his heart thundered in his chest. Fuck, he hoped she'd locked the door.

She leaned forward and her sweet lips brushed against the tip of him. He stifled a groan.

Then her hot mouth surrounded him and the groan escaped. Her gaze locked with his as she glided down his hard shaft. With her dark blonde hair pulled tight on her head and her conservative business suit, he could almost believe she was his secretary again. And she was in his office sucking his cock.

Fuck, this was hot. He closed his eyes as she glided deeper, imagining this was an ordinary workday when she was still his secretary and he'd called her into his office just to give him head.

She drew back, then glided deep again. Her soft fingers stroked his balls, which turned up the heat several notches. As her lips hugged him tightly, gliding up and down, his head started to spin and his groin tightened.

"Fuck, I'm so close."

She squeezed his base, then drew her lips from his erection, an impish grin on her face.

"I forgot to tell you, Jessica told me you have a meeting in ten minutes." She stood up. "Maybe I should stop now."

"Oh, fuck, woman!"

He pulled her onto his lap, and his mouth captured hers in a crushing kiss. His hand found her breast and he fondled it roughly, loving the feel of her nipple pushing into his palm through the thin silk of her blouse.

If he was going to make that meeting, he couldn't take this where he wanted it to go. But he also couldn't go into the meeting with his cock rock hard and aching.

He drew his lips back and murmured against her ear, "Well, you'd better get on with it, then. Now kneel down and suck my cock."

He rested his hand on her head and pressed downward. She sank to her knees in front of him again, then took his cock lovingly in her hands and stroked it. He groaned at the feel of her delicate fingers around him, then again when she captured his cockhead in her mouth.

"Oh, yeah." His fingers curled around her head as she glided deeper, taking his cock down her throat. Then she slid back and glided deep again.

Oh, God, he would come any second, but feeling the moistness of her delightful mouth around him made him crave even more. He wanted to be inside her sweet pussy.

Her fingers tucked around his balls and pleasure shot through him. She caressed them as she glided back and forth, taking him deep each time.

"No wait, I'm going to . . . Fuck!" He shot down her

throat, his pelvis jerking forward, intense pleasure pulsing through him.

She drew back and licked her lips. Damn it, he hadn't wanted to come in her mouth. He wanted to be inside her hot, sweet body.

"Stand up and turn around," he demanded.

She stood up and faced the desk, as instructed.

"Now show me what's under that skirt of yours."

He watched in anticipation as she wiggled her skirt up, baring her perfect, round ass.

God, it was so appealing. His fingers itched to glide over the firm, round flesh. Then to smack it, enjoying the sharp connection of flesh on flesh.

The urge to spank her, again and again, became overwhelming.

He stood up and cupped her ass, loving the feel of her smooth skin against his palm.

"You dare to come in here after you walked out on me. After I was a fair and generous boss. And now you want your job back?" He tightened his fingers around her firm flesh. He leaned closer and murmured, "The only thing you deserve from me is to be punished."

"Please, Mr. Ranier. Don't punish me." But she gazed over her shoulder with longing in her eyes, belying her words.

"Silence," he snapped.

He slid his hand over her smooth, round ass, then slapped it. Her fair skin blushed pink. He smacked again, then again, the sharp sound filling the office.

God, his cock was stiffening again.

He smacked a couple more times, then stroked her reddened flesh. He wanted to be inside her, pumping his cock until he exploded.

He stepped back.

"Open yourself to me and beg me to fuck you," he commanded.

His breath caught as she reached behind her and grasped her round cheeks, then drew them apart, revealing her glistening folds.

"Please fuck me, Mr. Ranier."

God damn. Her invitation acted like an electric prod. He grasped his aching cock, almost drooling at the sight of his secretary bent over his desk, her pussy exposed and glistening. Ready for him.

He positioned himself behind her and pressed his cockhead to her slick flesh, blood thundering through him. God, he thought he'd die with need. He thrust forward.

"Oh, yes," she whimpered.

Fuck, she was so hot and welcoming.

"Fuck me hard, Mr. Ranier."

He drew back and thrust again, knowing he was dangerously close.

"Oh, please, more," she begged.

He grasped her hips and kept thrusting. Suddenly, intense heat rushed to his groin and . . . God he tried to stop it but . . . The flood of pleasure spiked and he groaned as he released inside her.

He kept on thrusting as he filled her hot passage, then finally collapsed against her, his cock still nestled in her warmth.

But, damn it, she hadn't come.

He drew back and she stood up, smiling at him.

"Don't think you're getting away that easily." He pushed her back against the desk, then reached under her skirt and stroked her slick flesh, his finger finding her sensitive nub.

Her eyelids lowered and need filled her big, green eyes. He flicked it and she moaned softly.

He started to crouch down, but she grasped his shoulders.

"You really do have a meeting now," she said halfheartedly.

"I know." He captured her lips and plunged his tongue inside, thrusting the way he wanted to again in her pussy.

He lifted her onto the desk and knelt in front of her, then licked her flesh, slick with both their fluids. He drew her pink folds apart and drove his tongue inside. But his cock twitched and he realized he needed to be deep inside her again.

"Rafe, really. You're going to be late."

As his secretary, she had always prided herself on ensuring he was never late for a meeting.

He stood up and lifted her from the desk, then spun her around and pressed her to the wall.

"Fuck it. I'm in charge here." Then he drove his cock into her again.

She gasped, staring up at him with wide eyes. He grasped her wrists and held them over her head, then thrust into her again, driving her hard against the wall.

"Oh, yes." Her whispered words drove his need higher.

He rammed into her again. And again. Her slick passage massaged him as he filled her over and over. She whimpered and moaned softy, her eyes glittering with desire. Every beautiful, feminine sound of need she uttered, drove his need higher.

He wanted to know she was going to come. He wanted to hear her say it.

"Are you going to come this time?"

She nodded, her gaze locked on his as she pushed against the grasp of his hands, her body arching against him.

"Tell me," he said forcefully. "Say it."

"Yes, Mr. Ranier, you're—" She gasped as he drove in hard, slamming her against the wall. "You're making me come."

He thrust and thrust again, loving the sound of her whimpers. Then she arched against him and her whimpers turned to a rising moan. Her face glowed and her eyelids fell closed as she rode the wave of pleasure. He reached between their bodies and his calloused fingers found her clit. She gasped and moaned louder.

Then, incredibly, he erupted inside her. He lurched forward, crushing her to the wall. But she just kept moaning. His pelvis ground against her and she gasped, then collapsed against him.

They stood together like that for several moments, their erratic breathing slowly calming to normal. Finally, he drew back and gazed down at her.

"You've got your job back."

She laughed. "You'd be crazy to hire me back. I just made you late for your meeting. Probably the first time ever. What will the marketing department think?"

He chuckled. "Fuck them."

Then she grinned and raised her eyebrows. "Is that an order?"

He pulled her from the wall and smacked her bottom. "You are really bad today."

She giggled as she pulled her skirt down over her delightful cheeks, then headed to the door of his private bathroom.

"And that's why you love me." Then she disappeared inside.

His smile faded as he realized there was more truth to that than he wanted to admit.

Fuck, he did not want to fall for her. He'd just had a disastrous experience with Jessica, where he'd been so sure he was head over heels for the woman, only to realize it was just wishful thinking. He didn't really trust his interpretation of his own feelings these days.

And he didn't like what had just happened between them. At least, the way he had acted. Clearly, he still had issues to work out.

Melanie was nervous as she dressed for work on Friday morning. Today she had her three-month evaluation. She knew she'd been doing a fine job, but that didn't matter to Karen. The woman hadn't liked her from day one.

She took the bus to work, chiding herself that there was no reason to be nervous. The worst-case scenario was that she'd lose her job, and then she'd simply find another one. Still, she hoped it wouldn't come to that.

As she got off the bus, she saw Sue heading down the street.

"Morning." Sue tilted her head as Melanie fell into step beside her. "You okay? You look distracted."

Melanie shrugged. "I guess. I'm just nervous about my review today."

"Oh, right. Well, don't worry about it. You've been doing a great job."

Sue pulled open the door and Melanie followed her in.

The worst part of the whole thing was the waiting. Karen had scheduled her review for three in the afternoon, right at the end of the shift, which Melanie took as a bad sign. But when Karen arrived at noon, she seemed in a good mood, and the next few hours flew by as customers came and went at a steady pace.

Finally, the time arrived and Melanie followed Karen to a quiet table in the corner. Melanie sat down and Karen opened a file folder, reviewed whatever was inside, then glanced up at Melanie again.

"So, you started working here three months ago and, as you know, you've been on a probationary period during that time."

Melanie nodded.

"And you know that anytime during that probation-ary period, we can let you go without cause."

Melanie's stomach quivered. "We" meant Karen. She was the store manager and the only one who made the decision.

"For instance, if we find that you just don't fit in with the other staff."

Melanie knew the whole staff liked her. Except Karen.

Karen closed the folder and clasped her hands together on top of it. "Unfortunately, we have decided *not* to keep you on."

Melanie felt the color drain from her face and she had to fight hard to stop tears from welling in her eyes. She felt powerless and insulted, but she would *not* give Karen the satisfaction. Instead, she simply nodded and stood up. Then, feeling totally numb, she went to the back and re-trieved her backpack, then walked out the front door.

The limousine pulled up in front of Melanie's apartment building and Rafe got out. Melanie had called him that afternoon and asked if he would come over tonight. She'd sounded upset, but she wouldn't tell him what was wrong on the phone.

He was hoping that at some point, they could talk about what had happened in his office. He'd loved the fact she enjoyed role-playing and it had been exciting as hell, but he didn't like how he'd acted. The whole thing had left him sleepless that night, tossing and turning at the memory.

Why did he become like that? Controlling. Demanding. Almost abusive. He'd had to fight his obsessive urge to thrash her sexy, bare ass. And in the end, he'd rammed her against the wall and taken her hard.

She'd seemed to enjoy it, but he didn't like what it said about him.

Once at the door, he texted her and she buzzed him up. A few moments later, he got off the elevator and walked to her door, then knocked. She opened the door wearing a burgundy silk robe tied at the waist, then gazed up at him.

"Mr. Ranier. What are you doing here?"

He grinned. "Really? That's why you called me? Because you're horny?" He closed the door behind him. "Not that I'm complaining, but I was worried there was something wrong."

She stepped close and stroked the lapels of his finely knit wool suit. "Mr. Ranier, I just didn't expect you to show up at my house."

He smiled. Clearly, she wasn't willing to drop out of character to discuss it.

"Well, get used to it." He wrapped his arm around her waist and pulled her close. "I plan on being here a lot."

He captured her lips, then drove his tongue into her mouth. Hers glided forward, swirling with his. He pulled her tighter to his body, her soft curves crushed against him.

Then he released her. "Now take off your robe."

She stepped back and her fingers tangled with the knot at her waist, then released it. Slowly, she drew the fabric apart, revealing glimpses of skin and black leather. Then the robe fluttered to the ground.

His eyes widened at the sight of her in a black leather harness that covered absolutely nothing. Studded leather straps outlined her perky, round breasts. Her nipples, hard and thrusting forward, demanded his attention. A pair of straps continued from under her breasts downward and disappeared between her thighs, outlining her shaven pussy. Silver chains cascaded from the vertical straps, down the front of her body, while black leather straps continued around her back.

She backed toward her living room couch, then turned around and bent over the back of it, exposing her naked ass. The horizontal straps continuing around her torso connected to a single black leather strap appearing from her cheeks and attached to the strap under her shoulder blades.

His gaze lingered on her perfectly round, exposed cheeks.

"I assume you want to punish me, Mr. Ranier." She gazed around at him. "For making you late for your meeting the other day."

Melanie didn't know why she needed it so bad, but there was something about the idea of totally giving up control. Of being taken care of. She knew Rafe would never hurt her, so it was a safe fantasy to put herself totally in his hands. Let him decide what she did. Because, God knew, she couldn't seem to make good decisions in her real life right now. Submitting totally to him in their lovemaking just felt right. Somehow, she knew it would make this disaster of a day better. It would make her feel that her life wasn't a total mess.

Because under Rafe's guidance, somehow she would find her way.

But a struggle ensued in his eyes at her simple request. Why didn't he just smack her behind? He seemed to naturally take control when they made love. He had when they'd had sex against the tree the very first time, and then—her body quivered at the memory—in his office he'd rammed her against the wall, holding her hands helpless above her head.

With him, she could just relax and be his bitch.

She lowered her head and arched her back, enticing him.

"Melanie."

At his serious tone, she glanced over her shoulder again and gazed into his sky blue eyes.

"Look, I know you want to try new things, and I'm all for it, but . . ." He shook his head. "I'm not comfortable with controlling you. Or punishing you."

She stood up and turned to face him. "But it's just in fun. I know you'd never really hurt me. And you seem to naturally step into a controlling role."

He shook his head, as if denying it.

"Sure. Remember how you held my wrists above my head?" She picked up her robe from the floor and pulled it on, feeling exposed and vulnerable. "I found that very sexy."

"But I don't want that in our relationship." His jaw clenched. "To tell the truth, I'm not comfortable with how I acted in the office."

"But—"

He drew her into his arms and kissed her firmly on the lips. "When I make love to you, I want it to be sweet and loving."

She drew back, crossing her arms over her chest. "What about what I want? I like it when you take control. It's sexy and turns me on." The tears she'd tried to hide when Karen had fired her, welled to the surface. "It makes me feel cared for."

"Cared for?" He shook his head. "I don't get that."

"I don't care if you get it." She turned and marched away, not wanting him to see her tears. "Why isn't it enough that it's what I want?"

"Melanie." He stepped behind her and rested his warm hand on her shoulder. "What's this all about?"

He drew her around to look at him. She wiped away an errant tear. "I got fired today. I just wanted to give myself up to you. To know you would take care of me."

"By smacking you?"

She shook her head. "It's a sign of trust, I guess. Of knowing I can give myself up to you totally and you'll give me what I need." She slid her hands over the fine wool of his lapels, aware of the solid chest beneath.

"So if I don't spank you, I'm not meeting your needs?"

"No, it's more that when you take control, and there are consequences if I don't obey, it gives me a sense of you taking care of me. Sometimes it feels good to let go completely. But only if I have someone I trust watching out for me."

He sighed deeply. "We'll need to find another way, because I'm not comfortable with taking control of you. Especially with my abusive background."

She frowned. "But I know you would never abuse me."

He gripped her shoulders gently, his jaw twitching. "Look, it's not the time to discuss this right now. You said you just got fired. Do you want to talk about it?"

She shrugged. "It was the end of my three-month probation period. The manager decided not to keep me on."

"She's an idiot." He hugged her close and she felt warm and protected in his arms. "Do you know what you're going to do now?"

She shook her head, but not for the first time, thoughts of Travis' offer skittered through her brain.

"You know you can always come back as my secretary." He kissed the top of her head. "And imagine how fun that would be now?"

She gazed up at his smiling face and laughed. "Yeah. It would be so much fun we'd never get any work done."

She eased away from him and sat on the couch.

"Remember when I asked you why you didn't go out on the road with the band?" she asked.

"Yeah, and I told you I needed to be here." He sat down beside her.

"Are you sure you don't want to reconsider?"

He frowned. "Why? What's going on?"

"Well . . ." She fiddled with the sash of her robe. "When I was talking to Travis the other day . . ."

Rafe's frown deepened. "The day you went to get a gift for Jess, or did you see him again?"

Her teeth clenched at the implication that she was sneaking around behind his back, and she refused to allow this to turn into an argument.

"I'm not even going to answer that." But annoyance edged her words, despite her best efforts to hide it. "He told me that they could use another roadie." She gazed into Rafe's piercing blue eyes. "And he suggested I take the position."

She frowned at the flash of annoyance in his eyes.

"I'm sure that's not the only *position* he'll suggest you take."

Her chest tightened. "Are you implying he's only inviting me to tour with the band so he can get into my pants?"

"I told you he likes to steal women from me."

Her nostrils flared. "First of all, he can't *steal* me. That assumes I have no mind of my own and can't make valid decisions about who I want to be with."

His eyebrows arched in challenge. "And who do you want to be with?"

She sighed. "You, of course, but that doesn't mean I don't want to take him up on his offer. It would be a great opportunity to travel, and to really shake loose some of my ideas of who I am and what I should be." She took his hand. "And as I've said before, it would be wonderful if you would come back on tour. Then we could travel together." She gazed at him hopefully. "It would be a great experience."

"No," he said firmly.

Disappointment washed through her. "No, you won't come?"

"I've already told you I won't be joining the band again, and why."

She stared into his penetrating blue eyes and realized that wasn't the question he'd been answering.

She crossed her arms over her chest. "So you're saying that you don't think I'm capable of hauling equipment on and off trucks and setting up speakers?"

"I'm saying you're not going." His dominating tone set her teeth on edge.

She scowled at him. "You don't have the right to tell me what I can and cannot do."

"But that's exactly what you just told me you wanted me to do."

"That's different. That's role-playing in the bedroom."

He sent her a hard-edged glare. "It's as real as you want it to be." He tugged her into his arms and his lips came down on hers. Hard. He possessed her mouth, claiming her as his tongue delved deep. "You are mine and I intend to keep it that way. You will *not* go on tour with the band."

She gazed up at him in a daze, fighting her blatant desire to melt against him and obey every command he gave her.

But she knew neither one of them would respect her if she just caved in to his demands. She steeled herself against her weakness, and with defiance in her eyes, she flattened her hands on his chest and pressed him back.

"Think again."

Wild Ones

Melanie watched the scenery whiz by, mostly dense trees, as the bus sped along the highway. Once she'd agreed to go on tour with the band, things had moved pretty fast. They had been scheduled to leave the following week, so she'd had to hustle to get packed and tie up loose ends. Jessica had offered to handle subletting the apartment and had helped her pack up all her stuff and put it in storage.

All the activity had kept her mind off the fact she was walking away from her dream relationship with Rafe. At least, what she'd thought would be a dream come true, but had quickly come to a nightmarish halt.

She had refused to speak to Storm after their falling out, but now, with miles of road passing her by and little else to think about, she wondered how she had let it come to this.

"Hey, there." Diego dropped into the seat beside her. "You look deep in thought."

He and the other members of the band had been sitting at the back of the bus kicking around ideas for the upcoming show tonight in Washington.

"Not really. Just watching the scenery go by."

"And maybe thinking about a certain guitarist you left behind in Philly?"

She shrugged. She didn't want to talk about Storm. She didn't want to think about him.

She didn't want to *miss* him so badly.

"I thought you'd be sketching or something like that."

She gazed sideways at him. With his lips curled up in that charming smile of his, her heart began to thump loudly. Damn, she shouldn't be so affected by other men when she'd just ended it with Storm. Her heart clenched at the thought.

But the man had a point about sketching. It would be a great way to keep busy. Odd that she had no inclination at all to grab her sketch pad.

"I'm not really inspired."

"Well, *belleza,* anytime you want inspiration, I would be quite willing to pose for you."

With his dark, expressive eyes and his killer smile, a portrait of him could be very dramatic . . . or playful, depending on how she chose to approach it. But she could tell by his teasing tone that he was talking about posing nude.

She tingled inside. That could be inspiring in many ways.

She grinned. "It's nice to know I have a willing subject if I need one."

He took her hand and brushed his lips against it. "Yes, indeed. Do let me know."

Taking in the sexy glint of his eyes, she almost wished they were at the hotel they'd be staying at tonight so she could take him up on his offer. But once he got his clothes off, she wouldn't be sketching him.

Damn it, what was wrong with her?

Of course, she knew what was wrong. She knew as soon as she was alone in her hotel room, she'd start to miss Storm with a vengeance and then she'd question the wisdom of this move and begin to berate herself. And worse, reconsider her choice and think about returning home.

She wouldn't allow herself to wimp out like that. This trip was the opportunity of a lifetime. She'd spent her entire life allowing the people she loved to hold her back, and if she and Storm were meant to be together, then he needed to give her room to grow.

Diego reached under his denim vest and pulled something from an interior pocket. "I almost forgot. I have something for you."

He handed her a small package wrapped neatly in a red bandana, with a twisted blue bandana tied around it in a bow, like a ribbon. She pulled open the bow and unfurled the fabric to reveal a stack of small, white sheets of paper, a little larger than business cards, tied with a thin red ribbon. The paper was a good-quality, heavyweight artist paper with a vellum finish.

"Those are called ATCs—artist trading cards. You know about those?" Diego asked.

"I know the idea is that artists create original art on these cards and trade them with other artists, but I've never done it."

"I understand that the point of them is for artists to meet and exchange not only cards, but personal experiences. I think with you being on this journey of self-discovery, it would be good for you to meet with other artists. Find out what they've done, how they pursue their art. Maybe get ideas to help you develop as an artist."

She smiled at him and had to blink back a tear. He was so sweet trying to help her find her way.

"With us going through so many cities, I'm sure you'll get the opportunity to trade many cards and connect with a lot of fellow artists. I know that on the day we're in Savannah, that there is a trading session."

She smiled tremulously. "You checked that out for me?"

He shrugged. "You're a beautiful woman who is an artist. How could I not?"

He flashed her that stupendous smile again and her heart melted. Damn, she really was becoming a true addict when it came to these musicians. She never realized how soulful and intense they could be.

"Hey, Diego. We're going to do some jamming. You in?" Jimmy said.

Diego brushed his lips against her hand again. "As much as I would love to sit with you all afternoon, *belleza,* duty calls." Then he winked. "And I think this is a good opportunity for you to start creating some cards."

He stood up and walked toward the back of the bus.

Melanie grabbed her bag from under the seat and pulled out her small sketch pad and pencil, then pulled one of the blank cards from the stack and set it atop the pad so she had a hard surface to work on. With pencil in hand, she stared at the blank card.

And stared.

But all she could think of was Storm.

When the bus arrived in Washington, Melanie grabbed her backpack and followed the others to check-in, then they headed to the the Fillmore Silver Spring, where the band would be playing tonight, and she helped set up the equipment. As the band practiced, she set up a table with merchandise to sell during the show. She donned one of the band T-shirts, then with SAVAGE KISS emblazoned across her chest in frenetic red and gold letters, she sat at the table ready for the crowd about to flood in.

It was exciting being part of the show, even if it was sitting on the sidelines selling T-shirts. Afterward, the band joined her at the table to autograph CDs. When they finally closed up shop, it was pretty late, but they were all hungry so they headed to a restaurant for some food.

"So how'd you like your first night with the band?" Diego asked.

"It was exciting. You guys were great tonight."

Travis grinned. "So were you. We've never sold so many T-shirts. I don't know why we never thought of having a pretty woman sell our stuff before."

"Yeah, except most of the people buying were women," she said.

"Well, that's because they saw how beautiful you looked in the T-shirt."

Melanie laughed. "With your silver tongue, I would say if you were at the table instead of on the stage, we wouldn't have enough T-shirts to keep up."

The waiter brought their check and Travis laid down his credit card.

Melanie opened her pack and fished for her wallet. "How much do I owe?"

"Nothing. All food and expenses on the trip are covered."

"There are a lot of perks traveling with a rock band," she said with a smile, then tipped back her glass.

Travis entered the tip in the handheld device the waiter had handed him, then finished his transaction and retrieved his card. Even though the check had been paid, most of the guys still had full drinks in front of them, so would probably be staying a while yet, but Melanie was tired.

"Speaking of expenses, I was going to head back to the hotel. Should I just grab a cab?" she asked.

"I'm going, too. We'll share one." Travis stood up and pulled on his jacket, covering the snake tattoo curling down his bicep.

She followed him to the door.

Travis hailed a cab and they were at the hotel ten minutes later.

As they rode the elevator up, Travis leaned casually against the wall. She wasn't immune to his sexy, masculine presence in the small space. His layered, sandy hair brushed his shoulders and she could see the three gold hoops in each ear glittering in the light. A part of her wanted to reach out and stroke his whisker-roughened jaw.

"I'm really glad you joined us, Melanie."

She smiled. "Thanks. I think I'm going to enjoy it."

The doors opened and she stepped out. He walked alongside her until they reached her door.

"Good night," she said as she pulled her keycard from the pocket on her pack. But when she glanced up, he stood watching her.

"I really like you, Melanie. And you know I'm attracted to you."

Tremors rippled through her. And Lord knew she was attracted to him.

If she pulled him into her room right now, he would make sweet love to her and that would drive away the thoughts of Storm haunting her. For a while.

He stepped closer. "I'd really like to get to know you better."

From the gleam in his eye, she knew he was going to kiss her. Her stomach churned. As he leaned in close, she seemed frozen to the spot, but at the final moment her hand flattened on his chest.

"I don't think this is a good idea."

"Really?" He grinned. "I think this is the best idea I've ever had."

He leaned close again, but she shook her head. "I know you like to steal women from Storm, but I don't want to be part of it. I appreciate how supportive and kind you've been, but—"

He pressed his finger to her lips before she could continue. "Is that why you're holding back, because you think I'm using you to get back at Storm? Because if that's what you think, Melanie, you underestimate yourself. I'm interested in *you*. Got it?"

His hand dropped to his side but his big body still stood mere inches from hers.

"Thank you, Travis. But I still can't. I'm sorry."

"Is it Storm?"

She nodded.

"I thought it was over between you two."

She bit her lip and his eyebrows arched.

She shrugged. "I'm not sure," she admitted. "We didn't really sort it out."

"The guy forbade you to come on tour with us. And then he let you go without so much as a good-bye. Are you really going to stay with him?"

She gazed into his blue-green eyes. "I thought you were his friend."

"I am. But that doesn't mean I think he's perfect. Especially when it comes to women."

"Are you mad at him for walking out on your sister?"

"No, of course not." His gaze captured her. "But he did break her heart." His finger stroked down the side of her face, his gentle touch sending shimmers of awareness through her. "I don't want to see that happen to you."

No matter what he said, she could see it in his eyes

that he still harbored resentment toward Storm because he'd hurt his sister. Even though Jessica had found the man of her dreams. And yet the two of them had continued to play in the band together and socialize together. Men were funny creatures.

But now Melanie realized why Travis stole women from Storm. It was a form of payback.

The ding of the elevator doors opening made Melanie start and shift back slightly. She glanced down the hall. Diego was walking toward them. She stepped back, but not before Diego's keen gaze took in their stance and how close they stood to each other.

His lips curled up in a half grin as he approached.

"Hey, man, that's not the way to kiss a woman good night."

He stepped up to Melanie and before she could protest, he swept her into his arms and planted his lips on hers. The feel of his strong arms around her, and his hard chest tight against hers set her off balance. His tongue nudged her lips and she opened, then it swirled into her mouth. He tasted like sin and smelled like pure musky male. His hand cupped the back of her head and she melted into his kiss, struggling to draw in enough air. When he let her go, she was weak-kneed.

Travis laughed. "Here, let me try."

Then Travis pulled her to him. His lips captured hers and his tongue slipped inside her mouth with authority. His arms tightened around her, crushing her to his hard body and leaving no doubt about who was in control.

God damn! Travis came across as sensitive and gentle, but when it came to kissing he was all hard, authoritative male. Which made her long to know how he would behave in the bedroom. Would he dominate her like she craved so much?

All she had to do was say the word and he'd follow her inside right now. In fact, if she wanted to, she could probably be with both of them.

Oh, God, images of both men, hard and naked, made her tremble. She'd come on tour to learn about herself, but she'd never expected this to happen. This fierce awakening of her own sexual need.

Travis released her lips, but still held her tight to his body.

Melanie drew in a deep breath. "I can't do this. Not until I figure out what's going on with Storm."

"Well, do it soon." He murmured the words quietly against her ear. She doubted Diego heard them. Then Travis released her.

"I . . . uh . . . better go. I'll see you in the morning." She stuck her keycard into the slot and hurried into the room. "Good night," she said as she closed the door behind her. Then she leaned back against it, trying to catch her breath.

"Darlin', I think you're still standing behind the door, and I just want to say if you change your mind, my door is always open."

"Mine, too, *belleza*."

Travis chuckled. "I sensed that you like a touch of

authority from your man, and I want to assure you, I can give you exactly what you want. I can take total control. And if you like the idea of two men . . ."

Her breath held as she waited for him to continue.

"We can accommodate," Diego murmured against the door.

"Diego and I actually work very well together," Travis added.

Her heart thundered in her chest.

"Good night, Melanie. Remember. If you change your mind . . ." Travis said.

God, she wanted to pull open the door and invite them in.

But she couldn't.

At least, not until she knew where she stood with Storm.

Melanie walked toward the bed and peeled off her T-shirt then tossed it on the dresser. Seeing her half-naked form in the mirror, her black lace bra pushing her breasts up high and proud, she could imagine how Travis's eyes would darken if he saw her like this.

She scowled at her own reflection, then turned her back to the mirror and stripped down the rest of the way. She walked to the bathroom and turned on the shower. She washed her hair and scrubbed her body until it tingled, trying not to think of muscular, wet, sexy men doing it for her, then she stepped onto the bathmat and vigorously towel-dried her hair. With a towel draped around her, she grabbed the hair dryer attached to the wall by the mirror and dried her hair, then flicked off the light and returned to the bedroom.

She pulled on her PJs, then sat on the chair by the desk and grabbed one of the cards Diego had given her earlier. She picked up one of her artist's pencils and took a deep breath, then let the pencil glide over the surface. Allowing inspiration to guide her, she just went with the flow and let the form take shape. Finally, she put down the pencil and gazed at a perfect image of Storm staring back at her. His eyes intense, his expression somber. He wanted her.

God, and she wanted him. This little replica of him made her miss him even more. She pushed aside the card, then grabbed another blank one, but her pencil stubbornly churned out another image of Storm. She opened the desk drawer and swept them inside, along with her pencil, then slammed it shut.

She marched to the bed and climbed under the covers. As she stared at the ceiling, images of Storm, so hot and sexy in a tank top, tattoos along his arms and across his chest taunted her. She tugged down her camisole and gazed at her bluebird tattoo, then ran her finger along the outline, wishing it was Storm touching it like this.

Damn, she didn't even know if she still had a relationship with Storm. After she'd rejected his wishes, he'd probably written her off completely. He'd made no attempt to call her to say good-bye, and that had hurt. But then, she hadn't called him either. She glanced at the phone, tempted to pick it up and call him. To get a handle on where they stood. If she still had a chance with him.

But she'd known from the beginning that it wouldn't last. The very first time they'd been together, he'd told her he wanted a no-strings relationship. And why wouldn't he? The man could snap his fingers and women would come running. They'd even pull up their tops and expose their luscious breasts to him.

She had.

Even though he'd changed his tune and wanted to be exclusive, that didn't necessarily mean long-term commitment.

But maybe she could mend things between them. Her heart ached with missing him. She picked up the phone. If she just talked to him . . .

She stared at the receiver. But what would she say? If he demanded she leave the tour and come home, would she do it?

She shook her head. She couldn't do that. This was important to her.

So she should call Storm and confirm that it was over between them.

Unless it wasn't.

Damn, she felt like hammering the phone on the bedside table. She didn't know what to do.

Maybe she should call Jessica. Ask her advice. But she couldn't tell Jessica that she wanted to know if it was over with Storm so she could move on . . . to Jessica's brother. Anyway, Jessica would tell her to make it work with Storm.

She could call Sue, but Sue would just tell her to ditch Storm and go with the two hot guys on hand.

It's funny that she knew what everyone else would tell her to do, but she didn't know herself.

She sighed and put down the phone. In her gut, she knew she shouldn't be the first one to break the silence between her and Storm. He'd had no right to order her around. And he'd only done that because he didn't trust her, and that hurt.

A little guilt washed through her, because she really was tempted by Travis—and Diego—and she'd let them kiss her, but the joking way they'd done it . . .

Damn, she still felt guilty. Probably because she'd wanted so much to drag them in here and let them have their way with her.

But she hadn't.

And now she was suffering for it. Aching for the touch of a man.

She sighed and turned off the light, then pulled the covers around her. The sexual buzz humming through her made it hard to relax, or to forget about the fact that there were two hot guys ready and willing to relieve her ache at a mere word from her. She sucked in a breath and closed her eyes.

The phone rang. Melanie opened her eyes and reached for the receiver before it made that blaring sound again.

"Hello?" Her voice was hoarse from sleep and she realized she must have dozed off.

"Melanie, where are you?"

Storm's voice. The familiarity and warmth of it rippled through her.

"I'm in bed."

"Alone?"

She glanced around uncertainly, gathering her senses.

Then anger flared through her and she slammed the receiver down.

A few moments later, the phone rang again. She stared at it, fuming, but finally picked it up.

"Melanie, please don't hang up. I'm sorry. I'm being an idiot."

She pushed herself to a sitting position. "That's true."

"What I really meant to ask you is . . . are you somewhere we can talk?"

She wiped her bleary eyes. "Yes, we can talk."

"I didn't want to leave things the way they were. After you told me you were going . . . we never talked again."

She nodded and slumped back against the pillows. Where did she begin?

"Well, I want to travel with the band. Learn more about myself and what I want." She gripped the phone tightly. "I hope you can come to terms with that."

"If you come back here, we could figure it out together."

She gripped the phone tighter. "Or you could join us on tour. I already told you I know the guys would love to have you back in the band."

"And I already told you why I can't do that." His words were strung tight. "Staying here and supporting Dane in building Ranier Industries is important. Forging a relationship with my brother is important."

She steeled herself. "Well, this is important to me. And it's good for me. I've always stayed in a safe, secure little world as my parents trained me to do. With this, I don't know where I'll be after the tour, where I'll earn my income. And the guys are finding ways to help me to connect with other artists. Diego told me about an event in Savannah where a lot of artists are meeting up and he suggested I make connections and discuss how they're making a career with their art." She coiled her finger in the spiral telephone cord. "You know what it's like to want that kind of freedom. You sought it yourself. Please, Storm, I want you to support me in this."

"But, damn it, Melanie. I want you here with me."

And she wanted to be with him, but if he really understood, he would be there for her when she returned. She also knew that part of this aching need to return to Philly wasn't just to save the relationship, but a need to run away from this new challenge she was pushing herself to pursue. She wanted to return to a place where she felt safe and secure.

"Well, that's not going to happen."

She hesitated, knowing she had another challenge right now. She had to ask the hard question. She didn't want to, but it would be better to know the answer rather than be left guessing. Memories of Travis's insistent, commanding mouth on hers washed through her. Or turning down opportunities to move on out of ignorance.

She steeled herself. "So does this mean you and I are over?"

There was a long silence on the other end. Then Storm asked, "Is it what you want?"

Tears welled in her eyes. "No, of course not. I want

to do this, but I hope . . . I want you and me to have a future."

"You say that now, but with you there . . . spending so much time with Travis . . . Given enough time, I'm sure he'll eventually steal you away."

Her back stiffened. "You don't have a lot of faith in me."

"No, it's not that but . . . he's tenacious when it comes to stealing women from me. If he turns on the charm full blast . . . Damn it, Melanie, can you really tell me you are not attracted to him at all?"

She drew in a deep breath, remembering the devastatingly sexy kiss she'd shared with Travis less than an hour ago.

"I don't just fall into bed with someone because I'm attracted to them. Not if I'm in a relationship with someone else."

"So you are attracted to him."

She sighed. Obviously, that's all he'd gotten from what she'd said.

"Storm, do you really think I'd let Travis steal me away to punish you for hurting his sister?"

"Fuck!"

She could just imagine him raking his fingers through his wavy hair.

"All I can say is . . ." Storm began, "if he steals you from me, he really will be punishing me. He'll hurt me every bit as much as I hurt Jessica when I left." Pain filled his words. "More. Melanie, I don't want to lose you."

His heartfelt words reached into her and plucked at her heart.

"Okay, then trust me," she murmured. "It's you I want to be with."

When Melanie finally hung up the phone, she felt much better. Storm wasn't happy that she was traveling with the band, but he seemed to understand. And he seemed willing to wait for her.

Right now, lying in bed alone, she wished he wasn't so far away. She ached for him. She wanted his arms around her. She wanted to feel his touch.

After tossing and turning for a half hour, she finally got out of bed and went to the desk, then pulled out her pencil and an ATC. An hour later, she tossed two more cards into the desk drawer, both drawings of Storm. Big, sexy, handsome Storm. Totally naked. Yeah, these ones would have to be part of her private collection.

Morning came too soon. She glared at the numbers on the clock. Then she pushed the covers back and trundled to the shower.

Over the next few days, Diego asked her about her ATCs, reminding her of the artist trading card swap meet in Savannah. She didn't want to admit that she'd only been drawing pictures of Storm, most of them X-rated, so once she finished breakfast, she pulled out one of the cards and sketched Diego over coffee. The next morning, she drew a picture of Travis. She started sketching the band members on the bus on the way to Raleigh, North Carolina. After setting up for the show, she would sketch the guys while they rehearsed. She'd intended to sketch fantasy characters, which she loved doing, but the allure of the sexy musicians was too much.

But at night, in her room, she only sketched Storm. She seemed obsessed with doing it. And finally she decided it was okay to just give in to the obsession. It helped her feel closer to him, as if a part of him was there with her. And with all the practice, her technique seemed to be getting better.

The last night in Raleigh, she was working on a sketch while the band played. A woman who came to the table to buy a CD noticed her sketch and asked to buy it. Melanie was going to refuse, then realized this was exactly what she wanted. To sell her art. Another woman saw it and asked if she had any more. Melanie brought out her stack of sketches—the G-rated ones—and they were snapped up by the starry-eyed women who were so totally taken by the sexy band members. She laughed to herself when she imagined how they'd react to her sketches of Storm au natural. She could probably make a fortune.

After the show, they all went to a local pub. Jimmy and Dan played some darts with a couple of women and soon disappeared. Travis asked her questions about her art and smiled at her enthusiastic responses. An hour or two faded by as she and Travis and Diego talked and she couldn't help feeling close to them given the warm interest they showed in her and her art.

Finally, they headed back to the hotel, walking along the quiet streets in the warmth of the summer evening. As they strolled along, chatting and laughing, it almost felt like a date. Except she was with two men. Two hot, hunky men who played in a rock band. And who, right now, seemed to find her the most fascinating woman on the planet.

They reached the hotel and Diego held the door open for her. They stepped onto the elevator and rode it up in silence, Melanie intensely aware of their big, masculine bodies so close in the confined space. The doors whooshed open and she stepped out.

"You know, speaking of artwork, I'd still really like to see that tattoo you designed," Travis said as they walked down the hall toward her room.

"Is that so?" she said, arching her eyebrow.

"Absolutely." His gaze dropped to her breast and the nipple hardened under his not-so-subtle scrutiny.

She reached into her jeans pocket for her keycard. "I don't think it's the tattoo you want to see."

He gazed at her, his blue-green eyes simmering. "I know you're a talented artist and I really would like to see it."

Heat washed through her. "Well, I guess I can show you if you'd really like," she said, feeling a little wicked.

Travis' smile widened, then he gazed at Diego, who grinned.

"What about me?" Diego asked.

She'd almost forgotten he was there.

"Sure. You can both see it if you want." She smiled, knowing she shouldn't be so mischievous.

She reached her door and slipped her keycard into the slot. "Want to come in?"

"Fuck, yeah," Travis replied with a broad smile.

She pushed open the door and led them inside, then unzipped her leather jacket and slipped it off slowly. As she was draping it over the back of a chair, both men gazed at her with twinkling eyes, focused on her chest. She felt a little guilty toying with them like this, but she knew she'd never hear the end of their request to see her tattoo. And she had to admit it was fun.

She smiled, her fingers teasing the bottom of her black camisole top. The men almost seemed to hold their breath. Then she turned and walked to the mini fridge and pulled out a bottle of water she'd stashed in there earlier that day.

"Would you like some water? I only have one cold one, but one of you could grab some ice."

"No," they both almost barked at the same time.

Diego smiled. "We'd just like to see the tattoo."

She laughed and took a sip of her water, then she put it down and walked to the desk. She grabbed her sketchbook and opened it, then flipped through. When she found the right page, she held it in front of her, over her tattooed breast, and turned around.

"This is it."

The men stared at her, then at the picture of the bird.

To their credit, they did their best not to look totally disappointed, but they failed miserably.

"You didn't really think I was going to whip out my breast, did you?"

Diego shrugged. "A guy could hope."

Her lips curved up in a half grin. "Come on, guys.

You've know that I'm with Storm and being on the road hasn't changed that."

Travis stepped closer, a gleam in his eyes. "But Storm's a long way away."

She frowned. "But that doesn't mean I should cheat on him."

"Who said anything about cheating? My point is that if you're here, and he's back there doing whatever it is he considers more important, then maybe you two aren't meant to be together." He stepped close and glided his hands along her bare arms, sending tremors through her. "If you weren't attached to Storm . . ." A devilish smile crossed his lips. "Diego and I could show you some things that you'd never forget." He stepped closer, his face mere inches from hers. "We could bring to life fantasies you never even knew you had, but will wonder how you ever lived without."

Desire shot through her and her pulse pounded with the heat of the images he evoked. Like her sandwiched between the two men, their bodies in intimate contact. Travis' strong arms around her. Their hard cocks inside her.

She sucked in a breath, needing air desperately. Then Travis' mouth dropped to hers and his tongue glided into her mouth. Without thinking, she melted against him. She could feel his hard cock pressing against her belly.

Oh, God, she shouldn't be doing this.

The phone rang and she jerked back with a small gasp, then raced to the bedside table and snatched up the phone.

"Hello?" she said.

"Melanie, it's Storm. What's wrong? You sound out of breath."

"Oh, nothing." Her gaze slipped to Travis and Diego, her cheeks hot. "I . . . just got in and had to race to the phone." Well, it was mostly true.

Diego grabbed Travis' arm and nodded toward the door. Travis gave her a long, hard look, then finally turned and followed Diego. When the door closed quietly behind them, she felt some of the tension drain from her.

"Are you sure there's nothing wrong?" Storm asked. "You seem distracted."

She sat down on the bed, stroking a loose strand of hair behind her ear. "To tell you the truth, Diego and Travis were here. They just left."

"They were in your room?"

Her fingers tightened around the receiver. "Yes . . ."

She felt a surge of guilt at what had just happened, and wondered if she should tell him.

No, not now.

He'd freak out and torture himself for the rest of the tour. She would just have to make sure it never happened again. She could admit her mistake after she got home, but in the meantime, she didn't want to create any more strain between them.

"They wanted to see my tattoo."

"And you showed it to them?" he asked in a tight voice.

"Yes." She paused, waiting to see if he would blow

up. When he said nothing, she continued. "I have a picture of it in my sketchbook."

To her total surprise, he chuckled. "I bet they were pretty disappointed when you whipped out your sketchbook instead of your breast."

She couldn't help laughing, too. Especially since he'd phrased it the same way she had.

"I'm glad you're being so calm about it."

"Calm might not be quite the right word, but I know I have to trust you, or this won't work."

She smiled. "Good. I'm glad." She leaned back against the pillow and stroked her hand over her breast. "So, speaking of my tattoo . . ."

"Yes?"

"I'm touching it right now."

"Really?"

"Well, my top's in the way, but I could take it off."

"Definitely take it off," he said, his deep voice rumbling over the phone line.

"I think you should take off your shirt, too."

"That's a little inappropriate, since I'm in the office."

She smiled. "But having phone sex isn't?"

"If someone walks in on me talking on the phone, that's one thing, but if I'm sitting at my desk naked . . ."

"Naked, at your desk. I like that image."

"So what are you doing about it?"

She pulled off her top and tossed it aside, then drew the lace cup down and outlined the tattoo with her fingertip.

"I've taken off my top and I'm touching the tattoo now."

"Have you taken off your bra?"

"No, I've pushed the cup down. Do you want me to take it off?"

"Oh, yeah."

She laughed and put down the phone while she reached behind and unfastened her bra, then tossed it aside. She wiggled out of her jeans before she picked up the phone again. "I'm practically naked now. I'm just wearing a tiny pair of panties."

"Damn. I wish I could see you. We could Skype?" he suggested hopefully.

She glanced at her laptop on the desk, yearning to see Storm's naked body, too. "I don't have it installed right now," she said with regret. "Oh, but just a second."

She grabbed her phone and took a picture of herself, her hand cupped under the tattooed breast, then she e-mailed it to him. "I just sent you something."

She heard the click of keys, then he whistled.

"God damn, you're beautiful. You've got me so hard."

The thought of him sitting at his desk, gazing at the naked picture of her, stroking his long, hard erection, made her blood boil. She longed for that cock inside her. Her fingers slid down her stomach, then touched her slit. She was dripping wet.

"And the thought of your cock all hard and ready has made me really wet."

"Fuck, Melanie, I wish I was there."

"Is your hand around your cock? Are you stroking it?"

"Yes." His voice was tight with sexual tension.

She stroked over her slick flesh.

"Are you looking at the picture of me?"

"Fuck, yes."

"I want to see a picture of you."

But Storm swore under his breath, then said, "Hold on a second."

Really? Now?

"Dane, I didn't know you were still here," she overheard him say.

She covered her mouth in surprise. God, Dane had walked in on Rafe? Had he seen what he was doing?

Oh, God, had Dane seen the picture of her?

"I'm just talking to Melanie right now, then I'm going to finish up the notes for the meeting tomorrow." He was obviously still talking to Dane.

"Melanie, Dane says hi."

"Hi," she said weakly.

"Listen, I'll call you back. Dane needs to discuss something before tomorrow."

"I'd like to . . . but I need to be up early tomorrow. We're heading to Savannah." God knew she wanted to finish this, but she also knew a meeting with Dane would take at least an hour, probably more.

"Yes, of course. But I can't say I'm not disappointed to be interrupted like that. Can we talk tomorrow night?"

"Probably not. The show goes pretty late, then we usually go out afterward. That means probably after two."

"Okay, I'll try in a couple of days. But I'll be thinking about you, Melanie. About all the things I'd do to you if you were here."

"Storm, um . . . before you go . . . Dane didn't see the picture of me, did he?"

"Of course not. I closed it as soon as he came to the door. But believe me, I will be looking at it later."

"I'd really like a picture, too."

"Well, right now isn't opportune, but I promise I'll send you something soon."

"It's a deal."

After she hung up, she lay in the bed, frustrated and totally turned on. She stroked her breast, wishing Storm was here to touch her like that. She stripped off her panties and tossed them aside, then stroked her slick flesh.

As much as she tried to stay focused on images of Storm, she needed to feel a man's touch, so her mind kept drifting back to the feel of Travis' arms around her. Of his lips on hers, and his tongue exploring her mouth.

Storm was being understanding and attentive. And he seemed to have control of his jealousy. He was being everything she needed him to be.

Except here.

So when she touched her body to satisfy the aching, physical need he'd help build within her, it was actually images of Travis and Diego who brought her to release.

"So why aren't you there with her?"

Rafe glanced at his older brother across the conference table in Dane's office. "What are you talking about?"

"You should be with Melanie." Dane leaned back in his chair, staring at Rafe with that keen gaze of his. "Touring with the band. That's where you'll be happy."

"I thought you wanted me here, helping with the company."

"Of course I do. But you know, we can always conference call and interact over e-mail. I just want you to be a part of this company." Dane leaned forward. "And I want to be a part of your life. But I know you'd be happier being with the band." He smiled. "And with Melanie. I've never seen you as happy as when you're with her. Or talking about her."

Dane put down his pen. "Rafe, I know we're making up for lost time, but that doesn't mean the company has to be your only focus."

Rafe stared at Dane, barely believing his older brother was suggesting that Rafe go on tour with the band. His heart ached at the thought that Dane actually wanted Rafe to do something that would make him happy.

His whole life, Rafe had believed that Dane was just like their father, but he'd recently come to realize that Dane had simply had a different way of coping with their father's tyranny.

Right then, Rafe wanted to say something to let him know how glad he was that they'd reconnected, but he couldn't find the words.

"I'm glad you came back," Dane said, sparing him the trouble. "I know we haven't been that close in the past but . . ." Dane cleared his throat, then his eyes darted away as if he was uncomfortable. "You mean a lot to me."

"Thanks, man," Rafe said, then put his hand out. When his brother extended his, Rafe pulled him in for a hug and clapped him hard on the back. "I used to think you were like Dad, but I know now that's not true. You're nothing like him."

The next morning, Melanie finished packing her backpack and carried it with her when she went down to breakfast. She had an hour to eat before they got on the bus to drive to Savannah. When she walked into the hotel restaurant, she didn't see any of the guys, so she sat down at a table by the window and pulled out an ATC and pencil while she waited for the waitress to come and take her order.

"So did you and Storm have a nice talk last night?"

She glanced up at Travis' voice.

"Um . . . yeah."

At the curl of his lips, she knew he assumed she and Storm had had phone sex last night. He was right, but wrong at the same time. She certainly wouldn't tell Travis that it was thoughts of being in his arms that had finally given her the release that she'd craved. He already knew she'd needed that release because he had triggered her craving in the first place.

But let him think that Storm had actually satisfied that need.

He sat down beside her and signaled for the waitress, who arrived at the table with coffeepot in hand.

"Two coffees," he said. "We'll have bacon and eggs.

One order scrambled, and the other over easy. Right, Melanie?"

Melanie nodded as she poured cream into the steaming coffee in front of her. She breathed in the rich aroma, then took a sip.

Bam. Caffeine. That's the stuff.

Dan and Jimmy, the other two band members, walked by and stopped at the table.

"Hey, I heard Travis and Diego got to see your tattoo last night." Jimmy grinned. It was one of the rare mornings he wore his long, black hair hanging loose rather than tied back as usual.

"You know we're feeling left out now," Dan said.

She shrugged. "That's okay. I'll show you, too. As soon as we get on the bus."

"All right." Jimmy winked. "We could get on the bus now." His gaze dropped to her powder-pink tank top.

"Let the woman have her breakfast first, guys."

Dan shrugged. "If you insist."

"You going to join us?" Travis asked.

"No, we ate earlier. We're just here to grab a coffee." Jimmy held up his ever-present red metal thermal mug. "See you later."

They sauntered to the counter and the waitress filled up their cups, then they left.

"They're going to be disappointed when you get on the bus and pull out your sketch pad."

She quirked her eyebrow. "Are you saying my design is disappointing?"

He laughed. "Not at all. I personally love it." He stared at her over his cup. "In fact, I wanted to know if you'd design a tattoo for me."

"Really? What do you have in mind?"

"I was thinking maybe a wolf. Something dramatic with intense amber eyes."

She pushed aside the ATC and started to sketch on the paper place mat. "Just the face, or the whole animal?"

"Just the face." He watched her sketch out a design.

She quickly drew the shape of the face, then filled in the details.

"That is amazing. I don't get how you can just do that."

She shrugged. "I just see it in my head and let my hand go."

The waitress approached the table with their meals, so Melanie slipped the sketch out of the way and grabbed the place mat from the setting beside her.

"That's great." Travis pulled out his phone and took a picture of it.

"Well, I'll do a better version of it tonight. Or I could do a few more so you can have a choice."

"Nope. I want to go with this one." He tucked his phone in his pocket and started to eat.

After they finished breakfast, she went to the bus.

Travis sat down beside her. "You know, we'll be in Jacksonville in a few days. If you could finalize the artwork in time, I could have it done there. What do you think?"

"Sure, I can do that."

"And tomorrow is your artist meeting," Diego said from the next seat. "You all ready for it?"

She pursed her lips. "With people buying up all the ones I do of you guys, I don't have anything to trade." Because she sure wasn't going to trade the ones she'd done of Storm.

"So do some today, and maybe do something different."

"You're right. I'll do some fantasy creatures." As much as she enjoyed doing them, she hadn't done any on the ATCs yet.

Diego laughed. "I said do something different."

She glanced at him.

"Well, the women do fantasize about us," he explained.

It was true. *She* certainly did.

She laughed. "I meant magical creatures."

"Well . . ." His lips turned up in a grin.

"I get it. You and the guys are magical, fantasy hunks that no woman can resist."

Travis glanced around. "Except you, it seems."

His warm, blue-green eyes twinkled and she wondered how she had succeeded in resisting him for so long. Of course, it was because of Storm, but how much did Storm really want her? She was sure if she was really important to him, he could have found a way to come along on the tour.

"Except she showed you her tattoo." Dan stood beside their seat, Jimmy behind him.

Travis laughed and stood up. "Well, you'll get to see exactly what we saw." He smiled at her. "I'll leave you to your art." He moved to his usual seat farther back in the bus, where he usually worked on his music.

After she showed Jimmy and Dan the sketch of her tattoo, they acted devastated at not seeing the real thing and she sent them on their way, then got to work on creating some art.

The next morning, Diego accompanied her to the meet. They wandered around and chatted with various artists and she traded her three cards for a small watercolor landscape of a lake from a lovely older woman, a pencil drawing of a tabby cat by a younger woman who had a collection of drawings of felines, and an abstract in pen and ink by a bearded man. Everyone she met was friendly and helpful, offering different suggestions about how to make a career with her art. She felt exhilarated talking to so many like-minded people.

That evening at the show, lots of ideas tumbled through her head from the various things she'd learned from other artists about how they promoted their work.

When she got back to her room, she tackled her latest card creation with new vigor. But she still wound up drawing Storm. She tucked it into the special bundle and dropped it into the desk drawer, as she did in every hotel room she'd stayed at. She just had to face it. If she was alone in her room, she was going to draw Storm. She stared at the naked picture she'd done of him. If only he were here to model in person. Of course, if he was, the last thing she'd be thinking of would be drawing him.

"I've got an appointment at a tattoo studio in about an hour. I'd like you to come with me."

Melanie glanced up from her breakfast as Travis sat down across from her in the hotel restaurant in Jacksonville, Florida.

"You want me to get another tattoo?" She sipped her coffee.

"No, I'm getting the tattoo. The one you designed."

"Oh, right. I haven't had my coffee yet so the brain is not in gear." And she hadn't had much sleep since she'd been yearning for Storm.

"So, will you go? I thought you'd want to, since you designed it."

"I guess I could." It would be kind of fun to see her design rendered into reality on his skin.

Or so she thought until she stood in the studio and Travis grabbed his belt and started to undo it. She drew in a breath as he pulled back the strap and released the buckle, then let the leather slide through the metal frame. Her gaze locked on his fingers as he unzipped his jeans.

"Where . . . uh . . . are you getting the tattoo?" she asked, torn between spinning away, and watching in anticipation, as he lowered his pants and tossed them onto a spare chair in the artist's private studio room. She averted her gaze from his underwear and the outline of his intimate parts.

Travis just laughed and lay down on the table, then tugged down his underwear to reveal one side of his firm, hard butt.

The tattoo artist placed the template on Travis' muscular buttock. Melanie watched in fascination, and with a growing hunger, as the artist proceeded to bring the design to life on Travis' skin.

"Gorgeous," she said once it was done. And she meant more than just the tattoo. The man's ass was a thing of beauty.

Travis hopped off the table and gazed behind him in the mirror. "Nice job."

The artist covered it with gauze and taped it down, then Travis pulled up his underwear and donned his jeans. When they got back to the hotel, everyone was hanging out in Diego's room.

"Hey, there he is," Dan said. "So show us the new ink."

"Yeah, let me go remove the gauze."

Travis headed for his room and Melanie settled in a chair. Jimmy handed her a beer.

When Travis returned he grinned. "So you guys want to see?"

"Yeah, man. Bring it on," said Jimmy.

Travis stepped toward Melanie, with the guys behind him, then reached for his belt. Melanie's gaze locked on his buckle as he released it for the second time today in front of her, then began to unzip his jeans. As Travis began to lower his pants, a familiar voice cut across the room.

"Do you want to explain to me what's going on here?"

Melanie's gaze darted to the door to see Storm standing there. She jerked forward, spilling her beer on her jeans. She placed the bottle on the table and wiped at the denim, her cheeks heating.

What must he think?

And she didn't blame him. His gaze locked on her and she leapt to her feet and strode across the room, then took his arm and guided him into the hallway. She didn't let herself stop to think, just used momentum to steer him to her room.

Once inside, she closed the door.

"I know this looks bad, but there was really nothing going on. Travis just got a tattoo and he was showing the guys."

"And you."

"I'd already seen it."

He raised an eyebrow. "You've seen his ass?"

She sucked in a breath. "I went with him when he got the tattoo." She stared at his intense blue eyes. "I designed it for him, so he wanted me to go."

She took his hand and squeezed it. "Storm, that's all there is. There's nothing going on between Travis and me."

He stared at her for what seemed like a lifetime, but she realized it was only a couple beats of her rapidly pounding heart.

"I believe you."

The words hung in the silence as she stared at him.

"You do?"

"Of course. You told me if I don't trust you, then this won't work between us." He grasped her shoulders, sending heat pulsing through her. "And I intend to make this work."

Then he drew her close and lowered his face to hers. His lips brushed hers sweetly, then his arms glided around her and he pulled her tight to his body as his tongue slipped past her lips.

She threw her arms around him and held him tight as passion flared within her, and she opened to let him in. He swirled his tongue inside her mouth and she sighed, melting into his arms.

"Oh, God, I've missed you," he murmured when his lips parted from hers.

"Me, too." She gazed into his sky blue eyes. "So much."

And her body ached for him.

She stroked her hands over his solid chest, needing to touch him.

"Why are you here? Do you have business in town?"

He smiled. "No. I'm here to be with you. I'm going to ask Travis if I can continue on the tour with the band."

"What about your brother, and the company?"

"In fact, my brother pointed out that I should be here with you. That I can travel with the band and follow my heart, but still keep in touch with him on the phone and through e-mail for any major decisions. He doesn't really need me there to run the company on a day-to-day basis."

She stroked her finger down his hard chest. "Remind me to thank him next time I see him." Once she reached his belt, she tugged his T-shirt from his jeans and slid her hands underneath, then stroked over the solid wall of ridged muscles upward to his chest.

She found his nipple and ran her thumb over it.

He shrugged off his leather jacket and let it drop to the floor, then tugged off his T-shirt. He took her hand and placed it flat on his chest again. She teased his bead-like nipple with her fingertips.

The edges of his lips curled up. "You know, I have a hankering to see that tattoo of yours."

She smiled and stroked over her breast coyly. "Well, I've had quite a few requests to see it, but you should know that I will only show it to someone very special."

He smiled and slid his hands around her waist. "And who is this special someone?" His lips played along the base of her neck, sending ripples of pleasure through her.

"Well, his name's Storm." She grasped his raspy, square jaw in her hand and moved his face to hers, then planted a firm kiss on his sexy lips. "And I absolutely adore him."

Then she grabbed the hem of her camisole and pulled it over her head. She was rewarded with his heated, blue gaze locking on her breasts with a look of awestruck wonder. She reached behind her back and unfastened her bra, then lowered it from her breasts slowly, watching the desire flare in his eyes.

"God damn, I don't know how I stayed away from you as long as I did." His fingertip came to rest on her breast and he outlined the bluebird adorning her skin. Then he leaned forward and kissed it, his lips brushing the surface like the delicate brush of a rose petal.

She grasped his head and pulled him tight to her breast. He chuckled and she felt his tongue lap over her skin, then he shifted and his warm mouth covered her aching nipple.

"Oh, Storm. Yes."

He teased her hard nub with his tongue, then after a few excruciating laps, he sucked, and she whimpered.

"Oh, God, I've missed you."

He glanced up at her and grinned. "Me or the sex?"

She laughed. "The sex. Definitely the sex."

He swept her up and carried her to the bed, then placed her on it.

"Well, then I'd better get on with it." He unfastened his belt, then drew down the zipper of his jeans.

She sat up as she watched him push down his boxers, revealing his long—and very hard—cock. She slid to the side of the bed and reached forward to wrap her hand around his thick shaft. He stepped close and she stroked the impossibly soft skin.

"You look very tasty." She leaned forward and lapped her tongue over his hot tip. The salty taste of his precum flashed on her tongue and she opened wide and took his cockhead into her mouth. He was so big it made her jaw ache, but she squeezed him inside while she stroked his exposed shaft with her palm.

His fingers twined in her hair. "Oh, baby, that feels awesome."

She glided down his length, taking him deep, then slid back again. He guided her forward again, then set a rhythm she happily followed.

"Fuck, baby, I'm going to come." He tried to slow her down, but she pressed aside his hands and then cupped his balls and massaged them as she bobbed faster on his cock.

He groaned, then arched. Hot liquid filled her mouth. She sucked and stroked as he filled her, continuing her attention until she was sure he was done.

She drew his spent cock from her mouth and smiled up at him. "You really did miss me."

He drew her to her feet and kissed her thoroughly. "You know it." Then he eased her onto the bed and unzipped her jeans, then stripped them from her. He stared at her tiny panties. "Now let me show you just how much."

He tucked his fingers under the elastic and eased them down her hips, revealing her clean-shaven mound.

He smiled and stroked over the bare skin, then he pressed her legs apart and glided over her folds. She shivered at the exquisitely erotic sensation.

"You are so wet for me."

She stroked over his shoulders. "I want you so bad."

"Well, since you sucked me dry, you'll have to settle for this right now."

He leaned forward and lapped his tongue over her slick flesh. She moaned, curling her fingers in his hair and holding him tight to her. His tongue explored her opening, then he found her clit and teased it without mercy. As he flicked and cajoled, heat swamped her senses. She had longed for his touch and now he was giving her everything she needed. She lay back on the bed, moaning.

He slid two fingers inside her and sucked on her clit. As he stroked her inner walls, intense pleasure rose in her. It felt so good to be touched by him.

"Oh, God, yes," she wailed as she arched against him.

"Show me how you come, Melanie. I want to see your face in ecstasy."

The pleasure building within her exploded in an eruption of bliss. She moaned, her hands curled around his head as he sucked her sensitive bud. Reality melted as she catapulted to a realm of sweet all-consuming rapture.

Finally, she collapsed back to reality, panting for air.

Storm chuckled, then prowled over her. She had yearned for his big body over hers for so long, and now here he was. His hard cock nudged her opening.

"Are you ready for me, baby?"

She wrapped her hand around his big cock, now fully erect, and pulled him harder against her slick flesh. "I am *so* ready."

He smiled, then drove forward, filling her completely with one thrust. Her passage stretched around him. She squeezed him, welcoming his hardness inside her. And that act sent her over the edge again. At her gasp, he drew back and thrust forward again. Then again. She clung to his shoulders.

"Oh, God, I'm coming again."

She trembled as he continued driving her pleasure higher and higher.

She wailed, then gasped for air, then wailed again, as he kept pummeling her with bliss. She sucked in a deep breath and moaned long and hard.

Finally, she collapsed against the bed, catching her breath.

He nuzzled her neck, then rolled beside her. He pulled her tight to his body and she clung to him, resting her head against his hard chest.

"That was spectacular." She brushed her cheek against his skin.

He wrapped his arms around her and held her tight, his lips brushing the top of her head.

"As I said, I don't know how I stayed away from you for so long."

Storm held Melanie in his arms, not wanting to let her go. Her slow breathing told him she'd dozed off.

When he'd arrived and seen Travis pulling down his pants, standing in front of Melanie, his mind had jumped to the worst conclusion. Melanie had been letting her wild side free and who knew if she might harbor fantasies of having wild sex with more than one man. He might have been walking into the beginning of an all-out gang bang.

Jealousy had sliced through him, but he'd kept calm and given Melanie the benefit of the doubt. When she'd explained, he had believed her. She was clearly telling the truth.

But he still sensed something more. He knew Travis' effect on women and he suspected that Melanie was attracted to the man. She might want to be true to Storm, but if she had feelings for Travis, even if it was just lust, what would that mean for their relationship?

As Storm sat at the table eating dinner with everyone, he could barely drag his gaze from Melanie. Spending time away from the woman had opened his eyes to how much he cared about her. He'd thought he was in love with Jessica, but he knew he was in love with Melanie. But could he convince her of that? And now that Melanie was traveling and embracing her freedom, would she want to settle down with him?

When Melanie finished eating, she smiled at him. "I know you and the guys need to talk about integrating you back into the show, so I'm going back to the room."

She stood up and kissed him, a sweet brush of her lips, then squeezed his shoulder. "I'll wait up."

He held her hand. "You sure you don't want to join us for a drink first?" He was reluctant to let her go.

She shook her head. "I want to do some sketching, and I know you fellas want to catch up." She grinned. "And I'm sure having a female there will just cramp your style."

She turned and walked away and he couldn't help watching her delightfully swaying ass as she headed toward the door.

"She's a beautiful woman," Diego said.

Storm rubbed his chin. "Yes, she is."

"And very talented. You're a lucky man."

Storm frowned. "What do you mean, talented?"

At Storm's harsh expression, Diego shook his head. "Hey, man. All I meant was she's quite an artist."

Storm compressed his lips and nodded. What the hell was wrong with him?

He stared at Diego, who had a raw sexuality women seemed to love. It was one thing to trust Melanie, and he did, but quite another to get comfortable with other men noticing her. Wanting her.

"She's been creating these artist cards with her original artwork on them," Diego continued. "They're for trading, but people at the shows snap them up. I think we should have her do artwork for posters and album covers for the band."

"That's a good idea. I'm sure she'd like to see her work get that kind of attention and it would be good merchandizing for the band."

They paid for dinner, then convened in the bar. After their discussions about the show and how they'd fit Storm back into the tour, they sat back and enjoyed some drinks. After a few hours, Storm excused himself, anxious to join Melanie in bed.

"Hey, man. I'll go back with you," Diego said.

When they got outside, Storm hailed a cab and soon they were back at the hotel. Diego had obviously had a few too many. He swayed and Storm grabbed his arm to steady him.

"The elevator's over here, buddy." Storm pushed the UP button and when the doors opened, he steered Diego inside.

"Thanks, man. You're a good friend." Diego slumped against the back wall as Storm pushed the button for their floor, then Diego noticed his reflection in the mirrored wall beside him and jerked back. "Oh, that's me." He leaned closer and stared at himself in the mirror. "You know, I don't look so good."

"Ah, man, you're not going to hurl, are you?"

"Naw." He swayed a bit, then his expression turned uncertain. "I don't think so."

The doors opened and Storm guided Diego through them.

"You know, I'm so glad you're back." Diego threw his arm around Storm's shoulder. "We all missed you."

"I'm glad to be back."

Diego stopped walking. "I know you are, man. You're such a good friend."

"You said that already, but thanks."

"No, I mean it." He threw his arms around Storm and gave him a bear hug. "I love you, man."

Storm patted his back. "I love you, too."

Three people walked past them, giving them sidelong glances, as Storm extricated himself from the hold. He guided Diego forward again.

"Let's get you back to your room."

Diego's room was a couple of doors down from Melanie's. As they passed her door, Diego glanced at Storm.

"Aren't you staying in Melanie's room?"

"Yeah, I'm just going to get you settled."

Diego shook his head. "You know, she is so gorgeous and sweet and . . . *sexy.* I mean, it was hard . . ." Then he snickered. "I didn't mean *it* was hard, but . . . I mean it *was.*" He chuckled. "But I shouldn't be telling *you* that."

Storm's stomach tightened. He didn't like that Diego had noticed how sexy Melanie was. Though the man would have to be made of stone not to notice.

"Are you trying to tell me something, Diego?"

They arrived at his door. Diego fished in his pocket and pulled out his keycard, but had trouble fitting it into the slot, so Storm took it and opened the door, then handed him back the card.

Diego stumbled inside, then kicked off his shoes.

"I guess I am. 'Cause I feel guilty, you being my best friend and all."

"What are you feeling guilty about?"

"Well, for one, I kissed her."

Fuck, Diego had kissed Melanie. And he'd been worried about Travis.

"Then, there was the night she showed us her tattoo . . ."

Storm knew she'd only shown them a picture of it in her sketchbook. Or so she'd said. From the look in Diego's eyes right now, he was beginning to wonder what had really happened that night.

"Did you kiss her then?"

Diego shook his head. "No. I didn't." He gazed up at Storm. "But Travis did. And, man, they were both into it. It's a good thing you called right then, because I think clothes were about to fly."

Breaking Storm

Storm's gut clenched.

Heedless of his friend's rising anger, Diego gazed into space with glazed eyes, his lips turned up in a crooked grin. "You know, her tattoo really is beautiful. She's very talented."

"That's true," Storm said, his teeth clenched. "Now tell me what happened in her room."

Diego's gaze shifted to Storm. "Aw, fuck, you're mad now." He leaned forward in the chair. "Look, man, she really missed you. Don't get mad at her."

"Right now, it's not *her* I'm mad at."

Diego nodded. "Okay, if it'll make you feel better . . ." He pointed at his face. "Slug me. I shouldn't have touched her. She's *your* woman."

"I'm not going to hit you. Now tell me what happened with Travis and Melanie that night."

Diego shook his head. "I don't think I better."

Storm leaned forward. "It's too late now. You already let the cat out of the bag."

Diego's lips compressed in a frown. "I didn't mean to cause trouble." He sighed deeply. "Look, Travis figured that with you forbidding her to come on this trip and all, that maybe you guys weren't meant to be together. That she was just going to get her heart broken. You know, like with Jessica."

Anger and pain flashed through Storm. "Fuck."

"Man, the thing is, she didn't go for it. There was another night . . . before that . . . that I kissed her at the door, then Travis did, too. Travis turned on his macho thing and it was clear it excited her. If she was going to do something, I think she would have done it then."

Storm seethed at this admission.

Diego clasped his hands between his knees and stared at Storm, looking more coherent than he had a few moments before. "But she didn't. Man, she's into *you*."

"Yet you and Travis went into her room and tried to seduce her."

"You do know Travis is still angry at you for hurting his sister, right? You guys have never talked about that, but it's so obvious to everyone else. And sure, Melanie kissed Travis back, but she was lonely . . . missing you . . . and probably confused. She might even have been tempted. I mean, we both know Travis can charm the pants off most women . . . so you can't really blame her."

Diego stared at Storm. "But she really missed you." He grabbed Storm's shoulder and squeezed. "I'm glad you're back. You two are a great couple and I think you should do everything you can to make it work." His dark brown eyes grew intense. "She deserves it."

Storm quietly opened the door to Melanie's room and slipped inside. The lights were out, except for the one in the bathroom, which allowed him to see enough so he didn't stumble over the furniture.

He went into the bathroom and stripped down to his boxers, then brushed his teeth and headed into the bedroom. He set his clothes on the dresser and sat down at the desk chair by the window, then unzipped his bag, which sat on the floor by the desk, and pulled out his cell phone cord. He plugged it in.

He sat back in the chair. He still seethed at the thought of Travis kissing Melanie. And the thought of Melanie melting into Travis' arms, enjoying his attention, sent a sharp pang of jealousy through the pit of his stomach.

She was *his* woman and he didn't want her craving any other man.

He raked his hand through his hair. Fuck, he needed to get some sleep, but he couldn't bring himself to slide in beside her warm, delightfully feminine body right now.

Maybe he'd jot down some ideas he had for a new song. He turned on his phone, then activated a flashlight app, and pulled open the desk drawer for a pad and pen. A stack of papers, tied with a ribbon, caught his eye and he picked it up. He shone the light on the top one and . . . fuck, it was a drawing of a man. Naked.

He frowned and untied the ribbon, then glanced through them.

Shit, it wasn't any naked man. It was *him*.

It was his Savage Kiss tattoo. It was his face.

He continued glancing through the stack. All of them were of him. Not all naked. But most were. And there were dozens of them.

He glanced at her sleeping face and smiled. She may have been tempted by Travis' kiss, but clearly it was Storm she was thinking of.

Diego was right.

Melanie had missed Storm.

And she deserved to have his full attention. Not be left on her own, wondering if he was really going to be there for her. Wondering if the relationship was going to work.

Before Jessica, he'd never really had a relationship. In fact, he'd avoided them. His dad had really done a number on him, making him believe he didn't deserve to be loved, but he was coming to realize that he couldn't let his father's attitudes continue to control him.

He stared at Melanie. Her sweet face was barely visible in the low light, but he could make out her lovely features, so angelic in sleep. She was worth the chance.

Her eyelids opened and she gazed at him. Then she smiled and a crimp formed in the pit of his stomach.

"Hi." Her sweet voice was sleep-roughened . . . and so sexy. "You coming to bed?"

He smiled back and shut off the light app. "You bet I am."

He walked around the bed and slid in behind her, and wrapped his arms around her. She rolled toward him and kissed his chest, her sweet lips fluttering lightly over his flesh.

"I've missed you so much," she murmured between kisses.

He tucked his hands around her face and tipped it up toward him. "I know you did, sweetheart."

He covered her lips with his own and kissed her, showing her how much he cherished her. Her arms wrapped around him and she melted against him. His heart swelled and he wanted to lay her back and join with her in a sweet union of bodies. But right now, he wanted this more. This loving tenderness.

When their lips parted, he stroked her cheek. "I missed you, too."

The warmth in her eyes as she gazed at him warmed his heart. There was a depth of feeling that reached deep into his soul and tugged.

"Storm, I love you."

As soon as she said the words, Melanie felt him stiffen. Her heart pounded and she drew back.

"I'm sorry, I . . ." Her heart ached. "I shouldn't have said that."

She was a fool. Even though she knew that this was only a temporary thing—they were merely keeping each other company while they both went on this journey of discovering themselves—she still found herself believing that they might last. That he might come to love her as she loved him.

But at his reaction, that hope was shattered.

He frowned. "Melanie, I—"

"Please, just let's forget I ever said it." She had wanted to hear those words from him forever. Had dreamed of it night after night. But wishing didn't make it true.

He drew her close. "I can't forget it. I love that you feel that way about me."

"But you don't love *me*."

"Sweetheart . . ."

The sadness in his eyes tore at her heart. She fought back the threatening tears. He was here with her. At least for now. She should be celebrating that.

"It's just . . . I'm sorry, Melanie, I wasn't prepared for that."

"Don't worry about it. I was just being stupid."

"It's not that I don't . . . feel very strongly for you. But the only time I ever thought I was in love, it was with Jessica and it turned out to be completely wrong. If I believed that was absolutely real and it wasn't, how do I know this is real?"

She nodded. She had seen the love in his eyes when he'd talked to her about Jessica after he'd found her again. Melanie had believed he was truly in love with Jessica, too.

"Melanie, don't give up on me. I'll figure this out." He hugged her close. "I just don't want to hurt you in the process."

She reached up and stroked his whisker-roughened chin, loving the sheer masculinity of it.

"I want to be with you, Storm. I'll wait until you figure it out. Because no matter how you feel about me, I love you."

He kissed her, his lips brushing hers poignantly. Her heart ached at the sweetness of it.

"Baby, if I were to tell you right now that I loved you, you'd doubt it. You couldn't help it with everything that's happened." He tucked his finger under her chin and tipped up her face. "When I finally say those three words, there won't be a doubt in either of our minds that it's absolutely true."

"Hey, sleepyhead." Melanie dragged the tip of her fingernail over the leopard moth tattoo on Storm's chest.

Her fingernails were adorned with black-speckled aqua polish, one from the set he'd given her as a gift back when she was his secretary at Ranier Industries.

His eyelids opened and his gaze locked on hers. "Good morning."

The sound of his sleep-roughened voice, and the warmth in those sky blue eyes of his, warmed her heart. She wanted to climb right into bed, and snuggle in close. But she couldn't.

"The bus leaves in an hour. There's barely time for a shower and breakfast."

He grabbed her shoulders and tumbled her onto the bed, then rolled over her and kissed her soundly. "We'll have to make time for that shower." He grinned. "Because I'm a very dirty boy."

She laughed as he swept her into the bathroom with him, then stripped off her oversized T-shirt and panties and dragged her under the warm water with him. They got to the restaurant just in time to order something to take with them, then settled into the bus together.

"You two seem happy." Travis stood in the aisle beside their seats.

Storm gazed at Travis, keeping his smile firmly in place. "We are."

He nodded. "Good. Because I know Diego talked to you last night and . . . just remember. He'd had a lot to drink."

Melanie glanced from one to the other of them. "What's going on?"

Storm ignored her comment and said to Travis, "But everything he said is true. Right?"

Travis shrugged. "Yeah, I guess it is."

"So you and I are going to have a little talk later."

"I guess we will." Then Travis headed to his usual place at the back of the bus.

Melanie stared at Storm with wide eyes. "What did Diego tell you?"

"That he kissed you. And that Travis kissed you, too." He stared at her flatly. "And that you were tempted to do more, but you didn't."

"Storm . . ."

"Don't worry about it."

"I didn't cheat on you."

"I believe you."

She was confused. He was taking this too well. Last night, *after* Diego had told him, Storm had still climbed into bed with her and held her tenderly.

"You're not angry?" she asked doubtfully.

"I was at first, but I understand how it could have happened. And even though you let them kiss you, I believe you didn't do more." He smiled. "And I found the sketches in the desk drawer, so I know you were thinking of me every night."

He put a finger beneath her chin and gazed deep into her eyes. "And now that I'm here, I'll ensure that I keep your full attention."

After the show that night, Storm packed up his guitar then headed back to the dressing room with the others. Travis was sucking back a bottle of water. Storm grabbed a bottle from the cooler, then settled into the chair beside him.

Travis glanced at Storm. "Is it time for that talk?"

"As good a time as any."

Diego, who sat beside Travis, stood up and turned to the others. "Hey, guys, let's go help Melanie pack up the table."

Once the door closed behind them, Travis leaned back in his chair. "So, you got something to say about me hitting on Melanie?"

Storm compressed his lips and shook his head. "Actually, no."

Travis raised an eyebrow.

"What I really want to do is apologize to you," Storm said.

Travis frowned. "I don't get it."

"Look, man. I hurt your sister." Storm clasped his hands together between his knees and stared at them. "I feel bad about it and there's nothing I can do to change it. I wish I could." He glanced at Travis, who watched him with emotionless eyes. "I can tell you I walked away from her because I thought it was best. That I wasn't who she thought I was and . . . well, I didn't know who I really was. I was trying to figure that out . . ." He chuckled mirthlessly. "Still am. All I know is I couldn't do justice to loving someone else until I could love myself. And I couldn't even start to do that until I knew who I was."

"I don't get it. You're Storm. You seem to have your shit together, except for not knowing when you've got a good thing going with a woman. Other than that, you're confident, you love music, and you're your own man. You don't let anyone else define you. If you want to move on, you do." He shrugged. "What's the problem?"

"The problem is I'm not that guy." He interlaced his fingers and sighed. "I never told you why I moved to Philly."

"'Cause you figured out that's where Jess was. You went to get her back."

He shook his head. "No. I was there because that's where I grew up. That's where my life was before I hit the road."

"Okay."

"I went back there to take my place at Ranier Industries. My father owned the company and when he died a while ago, my brother and I inherited it."

"That's the place where Jessica and Melanie worked. It's owned by Dane, Jess' fiancé."

"That's right." Storm locked gazes with Travis. "He's my brother."

Travis tilted his head. "You're a Ranier?"

Storm stuck out his hand. "Rafe Ranier."

"Shit, man, you're a billionaire?" Travis chuckled and shook his hand. "Then you buy the first round of drinks tonight."

Storm grinned. "No problem. Does that mean I'm forgiven?"

Travis shrugged. "Sure. Why not? You're going to be my brother-in-law." He grinned. "And my sister did wind up with the better brother."

Storm laughed. "Yeah, thanks."

Travis leaned forward again. "Look, man. All kidding aside, I'm sorry I hit on Melanie. It's one thing to punish you by stealing groupies on the road, but another to go after Melanie." He shrugged. "You can't blame me, though. She's a great girl. But she obviously loves you. And you love her."

Storm took a swig from his water bottle. Travis' brow furrowed.

"Look, I don't even know who I am yet. I sure as hell don't know how I feel."

"Bullshit. You are clearly in love with Melanie."

"You say that, but I thought I loved Jess."

Travis slumped back in his chair. "Sure, but even I can see the difference. I thought you loved Jess, too. That's why it hit me so hard when you walked out on her. But when you look at Melanie . . ." He shook his head. "God damn, man. It's clear as day."

The fact that Travis was so definite about it gave Storm a ray of hope.

Travis' eyebrow arched. "You haven't told her yet?"

Storm shook his head. "I didn't want to lead her on like I did Jess."

"Ha. That ship has already sailed. Melanie is stuck on you, no matter whether you've declared your feelings or not. But you do love her, so there's no problem."

Storm sighed. "Last night, she told me she loves me."

"Shit, and you left her hanging?"

"I know. I fucked up so badly. But I couldn't say it because I didn't know it was true. Love isn't a word I take lightly. But, man . . ." He rubbed his hand across the back of his neck. "Yeah, of course, you're right. I do love her."

Travis nodded. "Okay, make some grand gesture then."

"Like what?"

Travis scratched his chin, turning thoughtful. "Let's think about this. What does Melanie really want?"

"She wants to find out who she really is. She wants to be free from rules."

Travis nodded. "And she wants you."

"Fuck, she wants you, too. And Diego."

Travis grinned. "Yeah, she does. But that's not an option."

Storm gazed at him, an idea taking shape in his brain. "I don't know about that. Maybe it is."

Two days later, a breeze fluttered through Melanie's hair as she laid the stacks of T-shirts on the table, preparing for the crowd to come. They were at the Delta Classic Chastain Park Amphitheater in Atlanta. There were other people setting up tables around her, some with merchandise for the other two bands playing this afternoon and evening.

Storm had told her he had a surprise for her after the show. Savage Kiss was scheduled to finish at about five or so, so it would be the first full evening they'd had to spend together since Storm joined the tour. She was looking forward to some romantic time together.

Once the show started, the crowd was energetic and enthusiastic. They applauded so long and loud that Savage Kiss had to play three encores.

Finally, it was time for Melanie to pack up, and excitement about the evening to come fluttered within her.

"Hey, you ready to go?"

She glanced up at Storm's voice. She dropped the last T-shirt into the box in front of her and closed it. "I just need to carry these boxes to the bus."

"Don't worry about that. Jimmy and Dan said they'd do it."

On cue, the two men appeared and started moving the boxes.

"Thanks, guys," she said as Storm took her hand and led her away.

"Yeah, no problem," Jimmy said. "Have fun."

Storm guided her to a waiting car with a driver. It wasn't a fancy limousine like he had in Philly, but it was a nice, comfortable vehicle with leather seats that she sank into happily after being on her feet for hours.

"So where are we going?" she asked.

"It's a surprise."

"Okay." She settled against him and, with the gentle motion of the car, soon dozed off.

She felt Storm's lips on her forehead. "Baby, it's time to wake up. We're here."

She opened her eyes to see his sky blue ones gazing down at her. She wrapped her hands around his shoulders and pulled him in for a kiss. He indulged her, the delightful movement of his lips on hers stirring a need within her.

"Are we going to a hotel room?" she asked hopefully.

He chuckled. "Not yet. I thought I should feed you first."

"If you insist." But her stomach grumbled, reminding her she hadn't eaten for several hours.

The driver opened the door, then she and Storm walked hand in hand into the lovely old inn. The restaurant overlooked a beautiful garden with a lake beyond. The sun set as they enjoyed their gourmet food, the flaming colors reflected in the calm water.

Finally, dessert came. She barely tasted the delightful chocolate mousse as she anticipated getting Storm alone in the room.

Once the bill was paid, Storm stood up and offered

his hand. A few moments later, they were alone in the elevator heading up to their room. "I must warn you, the surprise I have for you is a little . . . unconventional."

"But I thought the surprise was the nice dinner and staying in this lovely inn."

He shrugged. "That's just the setting. The real surprise is something a little more . . . exciting."

"And unconventional?" She smiled, curiosity buzzing through her.

The elevator stopped and the doors whooshed open. He led her down the very short hallway to a double door.

"This is the penthouse, so there are no other rooms on this floor."

She grinned. "So are you saying we can make all the noise we want?"

"That's right." His eyes glittered. "After all, I wouldn't want to disturb the other guests."

He opened the door and she stepped inside. She drew in a breath at the lovely surroundings. Bright and spacious, the suite was furnished with modern, but elegant, furniture in subtle tones. The wood was teak and the upholstery was cream and tan. He led her into the living room and sat down on the couch, then patted the cushion. She settled down beside him.

"Okay, so before I bring in your surprise, I need to explain something."

"About why it's unconventional?" She was bursting with curiosity.

"So let's start with the fact that I know you're attracted to Travis and Diego."

Her stomach clenched and she gazed up at him. Oh, God, why was he bringing that up?

"I don't want you to deny it, or apologize for it. It's reasonable that you might be attracted to other men. We're dating, but you're not dead."

She shook her head. "Where are you going with this?"

"The point is being with other men is only cheating if you're doing it behind my back."

Confusion swirled through her. "I don't understand. I don't want to be with other men."

"Look, I know that women sometimes fantasize about being with more than one man. Even Jessica once told me about a fantasy of having a threesome."

Her eyes widened. "I know. She told me you and Dane brought that one to life for her."

Excitement and disbelief rippled through her. *Oh, God. He could he actually mean . . .*

"There are a couple of reasons I set up this particular surprise for you," he continued. "One is because I know you are trying to connect with your wild side. To be free from the rules you usually allow to bind you. Also, I find the idea of watching you with two other guys extremely hot." Heat blazed in his eyes. "To watch them touching you. You getting turned on by them. As long as I'm there, that is."

"Are you really saying you've arranged for me to . . . uh . . . for Travis and Diego to . . ." She swallowed. "Are you going to watch us have sex?"

"Not just watch," he murmured. "I'm going to participate."

Oh, God. Three men.

She trembled in excitement.

"But . . . I don't really understand why."

He stroked a hair from her face and tucked it behind her ear. "Melanie, the idea of being with them excites you—and me—and I don't want you to deny what you truly want." He leaned closer, his sky blue gaze holding her transfixed. "And you know how the old expression goes. If you love someone, set her free. If she comes back, it's meant to be." He stroked her cheek. "I know you love me. And I trust you. If I allow this to happen, you'll be allowing yourself to truly fly, and I believe it will make our relationship stronger. I believe you will come back to me."

She stared deeply into his eyes. "Of course I will. I love you."

She pressed her lips to his and his arms swept around her, pulling her close. Her heart pounded as he kissed her passionately. Finally, his lips released hers.

"Are you ready?"

"I guess I'm as ready as I'll ever be."

He smiled. "Good." He winked. "Because I can hardly wait."

Storm walked to one of the doors in the suite and opened it. Travis and Diego stepped out and joined them in the living room.

"Hello, *belleza*." Diego's brown eyes glittered with excitement, while Travis smiled, his blue-green eyes intense.

She remembered when Travis had kissed her with a

potent authority and she wondered if he would take control again now.

"So you've decided to go forward with this adventure," Travis said.

She nodded, feeling guilty at the intense excitement in her, despite the fact Storm was the one suggesting this.

Travis stepped toward her. "I know you like a man to take control, so consider yourself my slave. Is that understood?"

Her gaze flickered to Storm.

"Look here and answer me," Travis demanded. "Do you understand?"

"Yes," she murmured.

"Good. And from now on, you will address me as Master. Now come here, slave," Travis commanded.

At his authoritative tone, she stepped toward him.

"Very good. Now say, 'yes, Master.'"

"Yes, Master."

The words sent chills through her.

"Now go and stand in front of Storm."

She walked toward Storm's seated form. His eyes gleamed as she approached him.

"Take off his shirt."

She unbuttoned his shirt, watching his solid, tattooed chest slowly become exposed as she unfastened each button. Then she slid the shirt from his shoulders and pulled it off.

"Kiss his chest."

She crouched down and ran her hand along his solid chest, the muscles hard as iron beneath her fingertips.

"Lick his nipple, then suck it."

She leaned forward and touched his hard nub with her tongue, then swirled her tongue around it. Then she leaned closer and wrapped her lips around him and sucked. His body stiffened and he drew in a deep breath of air.

"Now turn around and sit on his lap, then glide back and forth."

She turned around, facing Travis and Diego, and sat down on Storm's lap. Travis' face remained cool and commanding, but Diego's eyes blazed with hunger.

"Take off your shirt and cup your breasts."

She tugged off her top and tossed it aside. Diego's eyes flamed even hotter at the sight of her baby blue lace bra. When she cupped her breasts in her hands, she saw the bulge in his jeans grow.

She glided forward and back, pivoting her hips again and again. She could feel the bulge in Storm's pants growing, too. Heat grew within her as his fabric-covered cock stimulated her sensitive flesh through the thick denim between them. Storm groaned.

"Stop, slave."

She stopped, the ache pulsing inside her.

"Stand up and take off your pants."

A shiver ran through her as she stood, then faced Storm and unzipped her pants. He watched her zipper release, his gaze following her movements as she slowly lowered her jeans from her hips, then pushed them downward. When she stood up, she felt vulnerable standing there in a tiny thong, her naked ass exposed to the two men behind her.

"Now kneel in front of him and stroke his cock."

She obeyed, stroking down his belly, then over the huge bulge in his jeans.

"Is it hard?"

"Yes, Master."

"Good. Unzip him and pull out his cock."

She tugged the zipper down, then reached inside for the hot steel rod. She admired it hungrily as she drew it out. It was thick and hard, pulsing in her hand.

"Do you like it, slave? Does it make you hungry?" Travis asked.

"Yes, Master," she admitted, her gaze locked on the veins pulsing along the hard shaft.

"Take him in your mouth."

She gazed at Storm and her eyes widened at the hunger in his eyes. She leaned forward and pressed her lips to his tip, then widened her mouth as she wrapped her lips around his bulbous cockhead. It filled her mouth. She squeezed him inside, to his groan of pleasure.

"Drive him deep into your throat, slave."

She opened her throat and dove downward, his big cock filling her, then she glided back, unable to keep him that deep.

"Suck him."

Oh, God, this was so hot. All the men were fully dressed, except for Storm's lack of a shirt, and she was practically naked. And they were watching her bring Storm to climax.

She dove down again, then back. She wrapped both hands around him and stroked while she sucked his big cock. His fingers twined in her hair, coiling in the long strands and his breathing came in deep pants. He murmured little sighs of approval while she stroked and sucked. Then her hands found his balls, which she knew he loved, and she fondled them. He stiffened, then groaned.

"Fuck, baby. I'm going to . . ." Then he grunted and spurted into her throat.

She kept sucking, milking every drop from him. His fingers, which had tightened almost painfully in her hair, loosened and he slumped back in the chair.

"Fuck, I'm so hot." Diego moved behind her and drew her to her feet, still facing Storm, then slid his arms around her, his hands finding her breasts. "*Belleza,* I want to feel your naked breasts so fucking badly."

He released them, then she felt his fingertips play along her back and her bra released. He pushed the straps from her shoulders and the bra fell away. He spun her around and gazed down at her swollen breasts, his gaze locked on her hard nipples.

"God, they are so beautiful." Diego crouched in front of her and covered her breast with his mouth. She moaned as he sucked it sweetly, pulsing and teasing the sensitive nipple with his tongue.

She cupped his head and pulled him tight to her. He shifted to her other nipple and teased it mercilessly with his combination of licking and pulsing suction. She groaned in pleasure.

He sank farther, kissing down her stomach, then gazed at the triangle of her panties. He smiled up at her then hooked his finger under the elastic and pulled the fabric down, exposing her naked, hairless pussy.

"Diego, is she wet?" Travis asked.

Diego pushed his finger between her legs, and heat washed through her. He glided over her intimate folds, then pushed inside her slickness.

"Fuck, man. She is totally wet."

"Good. That's how we want her to stay. Slave, turn around."

Diego's fingers slipped away and Melanie turned around to face Storm again. Although his cock had emptied, it was already rising as he watched her.

"Lean forward. You can rest her hands on your thighs for support, if you need to."

She bent over, exposing her ass to Diego.

Diego slipped off her panties and tossed them away.

"Widen your legs, slave."

She placed her feet wider apart. Then she felt Diego's mouth on her ass, licking her smooth flesh. Then he nipped. A moment later, he licked her slick flesh. She sucked in a breath at the feel of his tongue rasping against her intimate folds. Two of his fingers slid inside her, then thrust slowly.

"Not too much, buddy," Travis said. "We want her begging for it."

Diego stroked inside her as his other hand found her clit and he teased it, sending pleasure swelling within her. Then he slowed down, and sped up again. He brought her close to the edge several times, each time backing off just in time. It was sheer torture. Sweet, delightful torture.

"Enough. Stand in front of her, Diego. And drop those pants."

A second later, Diego stepped in front of her. Her gaze locked on his long, slender cock, curving to the right. She grasped it and began to pump.

"Slave, I didn't say you could do that yet."

"Screw that. Let her keep it up," Diego insisted.

Travis laughed. "Fine. Go ahead, slave. Make him come."

She stroked the slender but rock-hard cock, wishing it was gliding inside her slick passage rather than in her hand. She squeezed tightly as she stroked, then pulled it into her mouth and sucked hungrily.

"Oh, yes, *belleza*. That feels so fucking sweet."

She pulled him from her mouth and nibbled the side of the shaft, then swallowed him again. She dove up and down on him, sucking him deep and hard. He groaned and she could tell he was close.

God, she wished he was inside her. She wanted to reach down and stroke her clit as she brought Diego to climax, but her Master hadn't given her permission yet.

"Oh, fuck, yeah." Diego jerked forward and hot liquid filled her mouth.

She sucked and stroked until he stopped pulsing, then she let his cock slip from her lips. She stood up and smiled. He pulled her into his arms and kissed her passionately, his tongue diving into her mouth.

"That was incredible, *belleza*. Thank you."

She smiled, then turned toward Travis, aching for her own release.

"Please, Master. I want to come, too."

Travis raised an eyebrow. "Really? Would you like me to fuck you?"

She took a step toward him. "Yes, Master. Please fuck me."

Her gaze dropped to the big bulge in his jeans, longing to pull it out and look at it. Then ride it to heaven and back.

"Come here."

She walked toward him, hungrily eyeing the crotch of his pants.

"So now I get to see your tattoo in person. Lift your breast and bring it close to me."

She tucked her hand under her breast and lifted it as she shifted close to him. He gazed at the mound of flesh only inches from his face, then his finger stroked over the bluebird. His light touch sent tremors through her. He stroked the body of the bird as though petting it.

"Did you look at this tattoo, Diego?"

Diego stepped close. "I admit I was distracted by other lovely sights. Let me see now."

He sat down beside Travis and his hot gaze swept over her breast. Travis leaned forward and his tongue glided over the tattoo, stroking it, then his mouth covered her nipple. Diego leaned in and took her other nipple in his mouth.

Her head dropped back and her eyes closed. "Oh, that feels so good."

Their hot mouths surrounded her, Travis sucking lightly on one nipple, and Diego swirling his tongue over the other. Then Diego began to suck, too, and she gasped.

She felt a hand on her naked ass and realized Storm had moved in behind her. She rested her head on his shoulder as his lips caressed her neck.

Travis released her nipple. "We're going to take this into the bedroom." Travis stood up and took her hand, then led her through the door.

"Storm, why don't you drop your pants and sit on the bed," said Travis.

Storm shed his jeans and boxers, then tossed his shirt aside as he sat down on the high king-size bed.

"Get him hard again, slave."

She knelt in front of Storm and stroked his semi-erect cock. He twitched as she swallowed his cockhead, and she felt him thicken and lengthen in her mouth. Behind her, Travis stroked her bare ass, caressing over her curves, then his fingers glided over her slick flesh. She groaned around the cock in her mouth.

"You want me to fuck you, slave?"

Tingles washed through her at his coarse words. With Storm watching her with hunger in his sky blue eyes, she nodded.

"I can't hear you, slave."

She drew the long, hard shaft from her mouth. "Yes, sir. Please fuck me."

Travis lifted her ass until she was standing, bent over with Storm's cock in her hand. He pushed her forward and Storm lay back as she slid over his body, until finally her chest rested on Storm's, the two of them staring at each other. Her hand still encircled his cock.

She felt hard, hot flesh nudge against her slickness. Not Storm's.

"Storm, I'm going to fuck your woman now. And I'm going to make her come."

The whole time, Storm watched her face, his gaze intense but unreadable. Travis eased forward, his cock penetrating her slowly, opening her to his hardness. Storm kept watching her. Her cheeks burned, excitement blazing through her. Travis kept on filling her, his seemingly endless cock moving deeper into her.

"Oh, yes."

Storm's eyes gleamed. His cock, still in her hand, was impossibly hard, betraying his arousal.

"Is he inside you, baby?" he asked, his voice deep and gravelly.

She nodded.

"Does it feel good?"

"God, yes."

"Squeeze me, slave," Travis commanded.

Her internal muscles tightened, gripping Travis snugly.

"Fuck, yeah." Travis began to move, his big cock gliding along her passage, stroking it. Then he glided deep again. "You're so tight and hot." He drove deep again. "Fuck, I'm going to make you come, and when I do, I want you to tell me it's happening."

"Yes, Master."

Travis thrust into her and she gasped. Pleasure swamped

her senses. He thrust again and again, driving into her with purposeful intent. Storm watched her face as pleasure rose within her.

"Oh, yes. I'm so close."

Storm pulsed in her hand and Travis rammed into her faster. Her insides melted and a joyous wave of heat wafted through her. Then pleasure spiked.

"Yes. You're . . . oh, you're making me . . ." She sucked in a breath. "I'm going to come."

The pleasure exploded within her and she moaned as Travis' hard cock kept filling her again and again.

Travis' hands gripped her waist and he thrust even deeper, then he leaned over her, his chest against her back, as his cock erupted inside her.

Her head fell against Storm's broad chest and her eyelids closed. Travis, now resting on her back, nuzzled her neck, then drew back. His cock slipped free of her body.

Then she started as another hard cock pressed against her opening. Diego thrust forward, filling her in one hard thrust.

"My turn, *belleza*."

Her eyelids popped open and Storm's blue gaze caught hers as Diego began pumping into her. She was still riding high from her orgasm, her tender flesh sensitized. Suddenly, pleasure blasted through her.

"Oh, I'm going to come again," she cried.

Storm's eyes, dark with need, watched her intently.

Diego thrust, then twirled inside her. Again and again he filled her, twirling and assaulting her body with pure pleasure. Soon she gasped, then moaned her release. Moments later, she felt Diego withdraw from her, leaving her feeling empty.

A moment later, Travis ran his fingers through her hair, tugging lightly. "I think we need to treat you to the unique pleasures of being with more than one man at a time."

He held out his hand and she took it. He led her to an upholstered chair across the room. He pulled it forward and turned it around so it backed against the bed, then he sat down. He held his cock pointed upward.

"Sit."

She faced Travis and positioned herself over his cock. He guided it into her as she lowered herself onto him. Storm and Diego stepped closer so they could watch as his big cock filled her deeply.

Travis nuzzled her neck, then murmured in her ear, "Let's give them a show to get them as hard as possible."

She cupped her breasts and stroked as Travis grasped her hips and slowly raised and lowered her onto his cock again and again.

"Oh, Master, that feels so good." She pinched her nipples, watching the heat simmer in the male eyes watching her.

Storm's enormous cock stood at attention. And Diego stroked his with an expression that was a mixture of pleasure and pain.

She leaned in close to Travis' ear and nuzzled. "Both their cocks look very hard, Master," she murmured.

"Good." He drew her forward then lifted her ass,

keeping his cock deeply embedded in her. "Storm, there's lube on the bedside table. Why don't you fill her ass?"

She watched as Storm picked up the tube and squeezed, then covered his cock until it glistened. Then he walked around behind her. Travis' hands grasped her buttocks and he drew them apart, then Storm's hard cockhead pressed against her back opening. Pressure built as he pushed into her. She pushed against him, relaxing, as his hard cock entered her slowly.

He was so big, but he eased in gently and she stretched to accommodate him. As he glided into her channel, Travis stroked her back, relaxing her. Once Storm was all the way in, none of them moved for a few moments, giving her time to get used to the feel of two cocks inside her.

Then she sucked in a breath. "God, this feels incredible."

"Room for one more?" Diego asked as he stepped up behind Travis, cock in hand.

She gazed at the red bulbous cockhead and smiled, then opened her mouth. He glided inside and she closed around him.

As she sucked Diego's cock, Storm grasped her hips and he began to move. As he drew her back with him, Travis' cock stroked her front passage. Storm guided her forward and back a few times, then he slid his cock along her back passage, pulling back, then gliding forward again. Travis and Storm found a rhythm, their two cocks thrusting in and out of her, driving her pleasure higher and higher.

She sucked hard on Diego, her hand wrapped around

him. He groaned and after a few moments, released in her mouth. When he slipped free of her lips, she moaned at the joyful sensation of the two big cocks still moving inside.

"Oh, fuck, baby, you're so tight around me." Storm thrust deep and groaned as hot liquid filled her.

At the feel of it, she catapulted over the edge, moaning as she flew into ecstasy.

Travis jerked into her, then grunted his own release. The two men twitched inside her, driving her orgasm even higher. She moaned and rode the wave, squeezing their cocks inside her.

Finally, she collapsed on Travis, her body aching from their erotic maneuvers.

Storm's cock slipped from inside her and he moved away. Travis smiled up at her.

"As slaves go, you're pretty spectacular." He cupped her face and drew her in for a long, lazy kiss. He stroked her cheek and smiled. "Anytime you want to try another fantasy, I'm at your disposal."

Storm helped her to her feet and swept her into his arms for an ardent kiss, his hot lips moving on hers possessively.

"I hope that was all you dreamed of."

She nodded, dumbfounded, and he smiled.

"And hey, Travis. The night isn't over yet. If my woman wants more of you and Diego, I assume you'll be at her beck and call."

Travis stood up and headed toward the door with a grin on his face. "We'll leave the door unlocked."

Both men left the bedroom and Melanie gazed up at Storm. "That was . . ." She shook her head, unable to find the words.

"Awesome? Fantastic?"

She smiled and nodded. "And incredibly generous of you." Her smile faded. "You're sure you're okay with what just happened?"

He kissed her, his lips lingering before he eased back and pinned her with an intense blue stare. "It made you happy, and you're still here with me. Of course I'm okay with it."

At one point, when Melanie woke up in the night, she felt a hunger for more. She stroked Storm's cock until he woke up to a raging erection. But rather than just taking her, he licked and sucked her to intense arousal, then summoned Diego and Travis from the second bedroom and all three men fucked her until she gasped in intense pleasure again. When she woke up the next morning, she was aching from the intense use of her body, and loving every bit of it.

The next morning, Storm arranged for room service and they all sat at the dining room table in their boxers, Melanie in a robe, and ate breakfast together. Melanie glanced around at the three handsome men while she sipped her coffee.

Yup. I have a definite addiction to rock musicians.

Melanie watched the scenery slip by as the limousine sped along the highway toward the next stop on their tour.

The inn had been an hour and a half drive roughly north-east of their route and they would be meeting the bus in a small town on the way to Louisville, Kentucky. Everyone sat quietly, each involved in their own thing. Diego leaned back against the seat listening to music, the cord from his earbuds dangling down his broad chest. Travis tapped away at his phone, probably texting or reading e-mail.

Storm simply stared out the window. Although Diego and Travis seemed quite relaxed, Melanie could sense the tension from Storm.

Did he regret last night? Had seeing her with the other men upset him? He'd seemed to be turned on by the idea originally, but maybe seeing her wantonness as she'd enjoyed the sexual attention of the other men had disgusted him. Maybe in the cold light of day he thought she was a dirty slut.

Her stomach twisted into a knot.

Or maybe . . . Oh, God, maybe when she'd told him she loved him it had made him feel too pressured. Maybe he'd arranged last night to push her away, hoping she'd want the continued freedom of seeing other men. Then he'd be the good guy by telling her he was fine with her pursuing other men and he would quietly pull away, hoping she wouldn't notice as she got more involved with Travis, and maybe Diego, too.

But the truth was, no matter how many sexy, virile men wanted her, they could never take Storm's place. She wanted him. And only him. Last night had been fantastic, but only because she'd shared it with Storm. And because it had turned him on, too.

She gazed at him, wishing he would turn his head and look her way. That he would give her a reassuring smile to set her mind at ease. But he simply kept staring out the window, watching the miles go by.

Storm got out of the limo and glanced toward the restaurant where they'd arranged to meet the rest of the band for lunch. He was glad to be out of the car where he could take a deep breath of fresh air. The vehicle, with its air-conditioning and contoured leather seats, had been quite comfortable, but after what the four of them had shared last night, he needed some distance from his friends.

The whole situation with the three of them sharing Melanie last night had been pretty intense. He had enjoyed it—fuck, he'd been so hot he'd thought his cock would explode—but it also left him unsettled.

The whole time they'd been traveling, he couldn't help thinking about how Travis had dominated Melanie, calling her slave and instructing her to call him Master. Clearly, it had turned her on immensely, and it had him, too, but now . . . Fuck, why did the women he cared about want a man to sexually control them? First Jessica and now Melanie. And the worst part was that he knew, deep down inside, he wanted it, too.

The limo driver opened the trunk and passed their luggage to the bus driver who stowed it in the storage area.

"Man, I'm starving," Travis said as he headed toward the restaurant door.

Diego followed him, and Melanie glanced at Storm

uncertainly. He hadn't spoken to her the whole trip and he felt a little guilty about that, but he'd had his own thoughts to deal with. He gestured for her to precede him and then once they reached the door, he opened it for her.

Lunch in the small diner was exceptionally good. Simple home-style food with large portions. The guys kidded around, and Dan and Jimmy talked about the two women they'd gotten lucky with last night. They kept it marginally clean in deference to Melanie, but she seemed deep in her own thoughts.

Soon they were back on the bus and Storm settled into the seat beside Melanie. She pulled out her pencils and sketchbook and flipped it open to a new page. He watched in amazement as she began to sketch a fantasy creature with wings, a big fluffy tail, and horns. It was dynamic and graceful, with a whimsical appeal. What surprised him the most was the enchanting personality the small creature conveyed. He almost expected it to bound off the page and dance around.

"That's sensational, Melanie."

She glanced up at him, startled, as if she'd forgotten he was there, then smiled at him, almost timidly. "Thanks."

He leaned back in the seat, continuing to gaze at her creation. "You told me about artist trading cards and how you can go to meetings to interact with other artists. Are there other things like that you're planning to do?"

Her pencil danced over the paper as she continued adding details to the little being on the page. "Well, Diego also told me about an Artist Battle."

He raised an eyebrow. "What's that?" He stifled a grin as he imagined two people armed with paintbrushes, one lunging forward and the other parrying.

"It sounds fantastic." She glanced at him, as if checking to see if he was really interested in what she had to say. "Artists have twenty minutes to do a painting. There's an audience watching the artists as they work, then at the end, they pick a winner and that artist's painting is auctioned off."

"Just the winner sells their work?"

Her brow furrowed. "I'm not really sure. Maybe the winner is the one who gets the highest bid."

Storm couldn't imagine working under that kind of pressure, but from the glimmer in Melanie's eyes, he knew it was something she'd like to do. "So when are you going to take part in one?"

She pursed her lips. "I don't know. I don't think I'm ready."

He gazed at her. "Why not? Your work is fantastic, and you just did that incredible drawing in no time."

She gazed down at her own creation. "Thanks, but the competition is painting and I couldn't just walk in there and finish a piece in twenty minutes without a lot of practice first."

"Okay, so what's stopping you from practicing?"

"Well, I don't have any paints with me."

"We can fix that."

"And it's cumbersome traveling with an easel. And then there's the time. You know better than me how hectic it is being on tour."

"You said you have to finish in twenty minutes. You can plan your project while you're on the bus, then when we get to the hotel, take some time before the show to do the actual painting. On days we have to start setting up as soon as we arrive, do your painting before you go to sleep."

She glided the edge of her pencil over the paper, adding more shading. "That will be hard with having to pack up first thing in the morning and all." She sounded doubtful.

"I'll help. You paint; I'll clean up in the morning before you get up."

She gazed at him, her emerald eyes wide. "You'd do that?"

"Of course." The fact that she doubted it stung a little.

She nodded. "Okay. Thanks." She turned back to her drawing and worked a little more.

He watched her a little longer. He didn't know why she was so subdued today, but he wouldn't be surprised if it had something to do with last night.

Finally, he settled back in the seat and closed his eyes.

His thoughts turned back to their erotic foursome and how Travis had dominated Melanie.

At least, he had only given her commands. Had her play the sexy, submissive love slave. It had been mild compared to what Jessica had wanted from Dane . . . and him.

Jessica stood before Storm, naked, her gaze cast down.

"Come here, slave," Storm commanded.

"Yes, Master."

Jessica stepped toward him and he pulled out his cock.

He flattened his hand on top of her head and pushed her to her knees.

"Suck it."

Delicately, she wrapped her hands around his cock, then her warm mouth covered him. He trembled with need. He wanted to drive deep into her throat. To fill her with his cock, making her swallow him whole. He drove forward and she gagged, but took him all the same. She sucked and he groaned.

He grabbed her shoulders and pulled her to her feet, then forced her back against the wall.

He pushed her wrists over her head and crushed his body to hers.

"I'm going to fuck you, slave. Deep and hard until you scream. Do you understand?"

"Yes, Master."

He nipped her earlobe and she yipped. "Do you want me to fuck you?"

"Yes, Master," she cried with such need he almost came on the spot. He pressed his cockhead to her slick opening.

"Storm."

"Call me Master," he gritted out, slamming himself into her so hard the walls seemed to shake.

"Storm."

His body jostled and his cock ached.

"Storm, we're here." Melanie's hand was on his shoulder as she shook him gently.

The dream images dissipated and his eyes opened. Ah, fuck. It may have been a dream, but his aching erection was very much a reality.

He shifted in the seat and willed his erection to settle down.

He hated the forceful way he'd taken her in the dream. It was okay when Travis took control over Melanie, but it wasn't what Storm wanted because he didn't trust himself not to take it too far. Like in the dream, where he'd taken Jessica too hard. It just wasn't right.

What if he tried to dominate Melanie and lost control there, too? What if he hurt her?

He'd never forgive himself.

"What were you dreaming of?" Melanie asked.

He just shook his head and stared out the window, watching the scenery pass by.

She placed her hand on his arm. "Is something wrong?"

At the concern in his voice, he forced a smile. "No, of course not. Everything's fine."

He just wished he could believe it himself.

After the show, Storm felt drained. Usually he was energized and ready to go. Unwinding was usually difficult because adrenaline still pumped through him, but tonight he knew when his head hit the pillow, he'd fall headlong into sleep.

As soon as they got back to the room, he stripped off his clothes, just dropping them on the floor beside the bed and climbed under the sheets. Melanie headed into the bathroom.

But as soon as his head hit the pillow, thoughts of Melanie lying naked beside him sent his cock swelling. Like pinning her hands over her head and driving his hard cock deep into her, while she gasped his name. Or her refusing, then him dragging her over his knee and smacking her ass until it was red with his handprints.

He rolled onto his side and threw his arm over his face. Fuck, he didn't want to want these things. The door closed and he felt her pull back the covers and slide into bed beside him. Her warm hand stroked over his naked back, then her delicate lips played along his spine, sending more blood pumping to his already aching erection.

He wanted to roll over and hold her down, overpowering her until she submitted to him completely, then drive into her like a piston, deep and hard again and again.

"Storm, are you asleep?"

Her words had to be meant as an icebreaker because she had to feel the tension in his body.

"No," he said, his voice slurred by his tiredness, "but soon."

He did not want to have sex with her in the strange mood he was in. With the primal cravings gripping him right now.

Damn, if he fucked her now, he might give in to those desires.

He might hurt her.

"Oh, I . . . thought maybe we should talk," she said.

Fuck, he didn't want to chance fucking her right now, and he sure as hell didn't want to talk about last night, which was triggering these disturbing desires.

"Pretty tired," he muttered.

Melanie stared at Storm's big, naked back, feeling very rejected. He'd barely talked to her in the limo this morning, but then on the bus he'd been so sweet, taking an interest in her art. When he'd fallen asleep on the bus, he'd clearly been dreaming about her, or at least about sex, muttering indistinguishable words in his sleep. But when he'd woken up, he'd seemed distant and cold. Then after they'd checked into the room, he'd muttered something about having to prepare for the show, even though there'd been plenty of time. He'd disappeared from the room, leaving her alone and needy.

Now he'd turned his back on her. As if he couldn't bear to touch her.

As if she disgusted him.

The next morning, when she woke up, Storm was gone. When she went down to breakfast, no one had seen him. She kept glancing at her watch as she ate breakfast with the others, then when she went up to pack, his bag wasn't in the room. Maybe he'd taken it to reception when he'd left the room earlier.

She dropped her bag with the others by the bus and glanced around, but there was still no sign of him, and they were scheduled to leave in ten minutes.

"Hey, Melanie, where's Storm?"

She turned at the sound of Travis' voice. "I don't know. I still haven't seen him."

Travis frowned. "His bike is gone."

Storm had arranged to bring his bike on the trip. He hardly used it—there was rarely enough time—but it usually remained locked in the rack on the back of the bus. She glanced back and it was gone.

"Have you tried him on his cell?" she asked.

"Sure, but if he's on the road, he won't hear it." Travis glanced at his watch. "Shit, we can't afford to hang around waiting. We've got a tight schedule today." He sighed. "Let's get on board so we're ready to go when he shows up."

Twenty minutes later, he still hadn't appeared.

"Okay, well, that's it. We've got to get moving," Travis declared. He signaled to the bus driver and he started up the vehicle and pulled away from the curb.

Melanie's heart clenched. When she'd worked for him, as Rafe Ranier, he'd prided himself on never being late, and that was one of the characteristics he'd kept as Storm.

There was only one explanation. He'd decided to walk away.

Even so, she couldn't believe he wouldn't have told Travis he was leaving the band. He might be angry and disgusted with her, but she was surprised he'd leave the guys hanging.

As they traveled, she stared out the window, confusion swirling through her. She knew she was just feeling insecure. Even if Storm had been angry or upset after their foursome, deep in her heart she felt he would talk to her about it, not just walk away without a word. That's not the type of man he was.

After about a half hour, Diego stopped by to see her.

"Mind if I join you?" he asked.

"No, I'd like that." She did not want to be left alone with her thoughts.

"How are you doing?"

"I don't know. I don't understand why he didn't show up."

"It's not like him, but maybe he needed to blow off some steam," Diego said. "Go for a long ride on his bike to clear his head, then lost track of the time."

She gazed at him, searching his warm, brown eyes. "He's been acting so strange." Her fingers twined together as she stared at him. "I think he's upset after our . . . uh . . . special night together."

He smiled. "It was special, *belleza*. Don't let anyone else's attitude make you feel bad about that. We all agreed to the experience and everyone, including Storm, enjoyed it." He smiled and stroked her cheek. "It was sensational. You did nothing wrong."

"So you think that's why he left, too."

He shrugged again. "I really don't know. He's been struggling with some shit for a long time now. Who knows what set him off?" He shook his head. "Just don't take the blame on yourself. Okay?"

She sucked in a deep breath as he sent her a reassuring smile. "Okay."

But it was an empty word. She couldn't help feeling that she'd driven him away.

"Yeah. I understand," Travis said into his cell as he walked along the aisle of the bus toward her and Diego. "Thanks for letting us know." He shoved his phone into his pocket, then stared at her with a grim expression.

"Melanie, that was about Storm."

Her stomach dropped like a rock. She stared at him, barely able to breathe.

"What is it?" she finally managed to utter.

"That was Storm's brother. Storm's been in an accident."

Perfect Rhythm

Melanie's chest tightened.

Storm was in an accident?

She sucked in a deep breath. "What happened?"

"His brother doesn't know anything yet, except that he had an accident on the bike," Travis said. "The hospital in Madison, a small town north of here, called him and he called us because we're nearby. Jess and Dane are on the way to the hospital now."

Images of Storm, broken and bleeding, flashed through her mind. A wrenching pain started in the pit of her stomach. She glanced around, feeling powerless.

"I need to go to the hospital, too."

"I know. I'm going to have the driver take a detour to Madison, which is about forty-five minutes from here, and drop you and me off."

She gazed into his blue-green eyes. "Do you think he'll be okay?"

"He better be. He's my future brother-in-law."

She just nodded. Diego returned with a bottle of water and handed it to her. She tried to twist off the lid, but couldn't seem to get a grip on it. Travis took the bottle from her and took off the cap, then handed it to her. She took a sip, her hand trembling.

She stared out the window, barely seeing the landscape flashing by as the bus drove onward. Worry gnawed at her. Travis squeezed her shoulder briefly, then left her to her thoughts, though he was a comforting presence beside her.

What would she find at the hospital? Would she get there and find out Storm was . . .

A lump formed in her throat. *Oh, God, don't let him die.*

As soon as the bus pulled up to the hospital, Melanie shot to her feet. Travis stood up and stepped into the aisle to let her pass. She reached for the overhead compartment to grab her pack, but he waved her away.

"I'll get it," he said.

She nodded her thanks and hurried to the front of the bus, Travis on her heels. When she stepped from the air-conditioned bus to the hot air outside, she drew in a deep breath, then strode to the hospital entrance. Travis opened the glass door for her and she stepped inside the cool building. It was a small hospital, with no one in sight.

"This way." Travis led her down a hallway with arrows indicating Emergency ahead.

Anxiety swelled in her as they followed the appropriate arrows, turning several times along the way, and soon arrived at the reception for Emergency.

Travis talked to the man at the desk, asking about Storm. When the man said no one had been admitted with that name, he asked about Rafe Ranier. A moment later, Travis joined her again.

"He said that Storm was admitted about a half hour ago, but they have no information on his status yet. They're taking X-rays. He said the waiting room is this way." He took her arm and led her through a door.

They stepped into a large area with stiff-looking vinyl upholstered chairs of metal tubing. The place was crowded, but Travis guided her to a couple of empty chairs and went and got her a coffee. He sat down beside her and she drank the hot liquid without tasting it, watching the other listless people in the waiting room, her own nerves fraying.

They had rushed here, her heart pounding the whole way, but hoping they would soon know how bad Storm was. But to have to sit here now, with no idea if he was horribly injured, or even dying, was tearing her apart.

Travis took her hand in his and squeezed it, offering some small level of comfort. She gazed at him, trying to stop tears from welling in her eyes. He just gazed back at her, both of them knowing there was nothing to say. Thankfully, he didn't try to make small talk. He was just a comforting presence by her side. Hours passed, her stomach churning and her nerves shot. Melanie didn't know how much more she could take.

"Melanie."

Melanie glanced up and saw Jessica hurrying toward her.

Melanie stood and stepped forward to meet her with open arms.

"Oh, Melanie. I'm glad you're here." Jessica wrapped her arms around Melanie and hugged her tightly.

Instead of a quick hug, she hung on. Melanie patted her back. Jessica and Storm might not be a couple any longer, but they had been in love once and Melanie knew Jessica still cared deeply about him. Finally, Jessica released her, then she glanced at Travis and hugged him.

"Hey, sis." He didn't ask any questions, just held her tight.

Dane stepped toward Melanie.

"Mr. Ranier, I'm so sorry—"

"I'm Dane," he said and to her total surprise, he took her in his arms and hugged her tight. He was so big and warm and comforting she could have broken down into tears right then and there.

One of his hands rested flat on the middle of her back, and it had a calming effect on her.

"I know you must be worried, Melanie. We all are. But I know he'll be all right."

"How do you . . . ?" Her throat was so tight, her voice turned to a croak and she started again. "How do you know?"

He drew back and gazed at her with confidence. "Because I'm not willing to lose him again."

She stared into his confident blue eyes and couldn't help but believe him. The man always got what he wanted, so even though it defied logic, she believed that he would not be denied this.

"The man at reception told us they couldn't give us any information about Storm's condition until his family arrived," Travis said. "All we know is that they were taking X-rays. Do you know any more than that?"

"I'm afraid not," Dane answered.

"Can you go in and see him?" Melanie asked. "You're family so they'll let you, right?"

"No, they won't. I already asked," Dane answered.

Oh, God, was Storm so bad that . . . She choked up, not willing to continue that line of thinking.

"Do you know anything about the accident?" Travis asked.

"I did talk to the police." Dane glanced at Melanie.

At his hesitation, her heart froze.

"What is it?" Melanie glanced from Dane to Jessica, pleading in her eyes.

Jessica took her hand. "Look, we don't really know."

"But . . . it's bad, isn't it?"

Their silence confirmed it.

Melanie wrung her hands together and Travis guided her to a chair. She sank into it and Jessica sat beside her.

"Would you like some coffee?" Dane asked.

Melanie shook her head. "I've had enough coffee."

"Some water then?"

She nodded.

"Jess?" he asked.

"Water, too."

He glanced toward Travis.

"I'll come with you," Travis said, and the two of them headed for the door.

Melanie bit her lip and gazed at Jessica.

"I know what's on your mind," Jessica said. "The same thing as me. Is he okay? He's alive, but . . . is he paralyzed? Is he still in one piece? Is he . . ." Her voice broke and she wiped at her eyes. "I'm sorry. I'm so sorry, Melanie. I shouldn't say those things. But it's what we're both afraid of." She squeezed Melanie's hand. "I should be strong for you. I shouldn't say things that will upset you."

"It's okay. I know what you mean and maybe it's better that we express our fears."

Travis reappeared with three water bottles and handed one to each of them, then sat on the other chair beside Jessica.

"Where's Dane?" Jessica asked.

"A nurse spotted us and told Dane that he could go in to see Storm."

Jessica's face lit up. "Oh, that's wonderful. That's a good sign, right?"

A wave of relief washed through Melanie, until she noticed Travis's grim expression, then her gut tightened.

"She said they're worried about his spine and the X-rays were inconclusive, so they're sending him for a CT scan."

"What does that mean? What else did she say?" Melanie asked.

He shook his head. "Nothing else. We'll have to wait for Dane to get back. Once he sees him, and talks to him, we'll know more."

Melanie just nodded like a bobblehead doll.

"I'm afraid it might be a while, though," Travis continued.

Melanie suddenly found the room stifling. She pushed herself to her feet. "I need to get some air."

"I'll come with you." Travis stood up, but she shook her head.

"You stay with your sister. I'll be okay." Melanie hurried to the door and stepped into the hallway. She turned left and walked, no idea where she was going.

"Melanie, wait."

At Travis's voice, she turned around.

He caught up with her. "I don't want to leave you alone just wandering around the hospital. I'll walk with you."

"Really, I'm okay, I—"

A man in green scrubs passed them pushing a patient on a gurney. The man was flat on his back and was strapped down, totally immobilized. It was a distressing sight and . . .

Her eyes widened. "Oh, God. That's Storm."

His eyes were closed and he looked shockingly pale.

She started forward, to follow the gurney that was already several yards away, but Travis grasped her arm.

"No, Melanie. Come back with me."

She gazed at him, pleadingly. "But I have to—"

"No," he said in a no-nonsense tone, then his voice softened. "Let's go back to the waiting room. Maybe Dane is there with more information."

She watched Storm and the orderly disappear through a door at the end of the hall, and she bit her lip, then finally nodded and allowed Travis to guide her back.

Dane was sitting with Jessica and they glanced up when Melanie and Travis returned.

"I'm just heading over to sit with Rafe while he waits for the CT scan," Dane said, "but I came out to update you before I go. He's regained consciousness and appears to be in one piece. He is in some pain, so they're checking for internal injuries."

"Why do they have him strapped down like that?" Melanie asked.

Dane's gaze darted to her face.

"We saw him being wheeled down the hallway," Travis explained.

Dane nodded. "They told me that's because they don't know if he's suffered a spinal injury so they want to keep him immobile until they find out."

Melanie sank into the chair, wishing this nightmare was over. After a few minutes, Dane left to be with Storm and the three of them sat in silence. It seemed hours before Dane finally returned.

"What's happened?" Jessica asked as he sat down.

"I still don't know, but they said they'll call me soon to go over the results. In the meantime, Rafe sent me back out here. He knew you'd all be worried."

Dane took Melanie's hand and gazed at her. "He said to tell you he'll be fine."

She nodded. Storm's comforting words didn't mean anything—the test results would tell them if he really was fine or not—but she liked that he knew she was here for him.

"Mr. Ranier?"

Melanie and the others glanced toward the tall man in scrubs across the room who had called Dane's name.

Dane stood up and followed the doctor from the waiting room.

Travis leaned forward, intertwining his fingers. "I guess we'll know soon."

Soon turned out to be about a half hour.

"Rafe!" Jessica surged to her feet and Melanie glanced after her to see Dane pushing a wheelchair.

Storm sat in the chair, still pale, with a badly bruised cheek and a black eye, but with no casts in sight. Joy surged through Melanie as she stood and walked toward them, holding back a little while Jessica gushed over him. Travis stood beside Melanie and placed his hand on her shoulder and squeezed. She fought back the tears of relief.

Jessica moved beside the chair and Melanie stepped forward.

"You gave us quite a scare," she said.

"I know. I'm sorry."

His voice sounded shaky.

"I'm just glad you're okay."

Their gazes locked for a second, then he seemed to fade into a daze.

"He's pretty bashed up and has some nasty bruises. He's on painkillers right now," Dane said. "Let's get him home."

———

Melanie watched the door close behind Jessica and Dane, then she returned to Storm's bedroom and sat in the upholstered chair by the window. Storm was asleep.

Dane had arranged transportation to take Travis to meet the band so he could do the show tonight. The doctor had told Storm to take it easy for a week or two, then he could return to work.

She gazed at him, his eyes closed, his broad shoulders naked above the dove gray sheets, tattooed arms sprawled to the side.

She'd faced losing him today, at first because she'd believed he'd up and left her, then because she thought he'd been taken from her in an accident. Her heart ached at the thought of not having him in her life anymore.

But that might still happen. She had no idea why he'd gotten up this morning and taken off on his bike, but she had the sick feeling he had decided the two of them weren't meant to be together. Whether he'd wanted time to think to figure out the gentlest way to break up with her, or whether he'd decided to just up and leave, she wasn't sure. The latter wasn't really his style—he was more caring than that—so he'd probably been trying to figure a way out of the relationship. With her traveling with the band, there wasn't a straightforward answer. Since he felt guilty about her leaving Ranier Industries because of him, she knew he would be unhappy driving her away from this job with the band, too, yet if he wanted to keep playing with them, it would be awkward if they broke up.

Damn it, was it possible he might pretend to keep the relationship going until the end of the tour, but keep a growing distance between them until both of them would be ready to end it?

She blinked back a tear at the thought he didn't really want her, and that she would probably lose him soon.

Storm drifted toward consciousness, feeling sluggish. He should open his eyes, but his lids felt too heavy to budge.

He realized he wasn't quite sure where he was. He should be in a hotel room on tour, but from the feel of the high-quality pillow-top mattress under him and the fine Egyptian cotton sheets around him, he would guess this was his bedroom in his Philly penthouse.

He drew in a breath and opened his eyes, then blinked at the sunshine streaming across his face. He pushed himself up on his elbows, but pain shot through him and he groaned. His head ached and his whole body felt bruised and mistreated.

"Hi."

He turned his head to see Melanie sitting in the armchair a couple of yards from the bed. She sat in a tight little ball, hugging her knees close to her body.

"Hi." He rested his hand on his head, wishing the pounding inside would stop.

"Do you want another painkiller?" Melanie asked, concern in her wide green eyes as she sat forward, dropping her feet to the floor. "I'll get you some fresh water."

"No." He waved his hand. "No painkillers." He started to sit up again, slowly this time. Everything ached, especially his ribs, but there was no intense, shooting pain this time. Or maybe he was just getting used to it.

She rushed to his side and propped some pillows behind him. He rested back against them, deciding he'd give himself a moment before he pushed himself to his feet and answered the call of nature.

"Do you remember the accident?" she asked, standing beside him, watching his face.

Accident?

"Ah, fuck yeah." Memories of swerving and his bike going out of control, then him flying through the air. "Damn. Did the deer make it?"

"Deer? I don't know. Is that how it happened? You almost got killed trying to avoid a deer?"

He shrugged, then wished he hadn't at the spike of pain through his shoulders. "Actually, the car in front of me swerved to miss the deer and went out of control."

"But the police told Dane there were no other vehicles around. If the driver wasn't hurt, why wouldn't he stay with you?"

"I'm pretty sure he'd been drinking. He'd been driving erratically and I'd been watching for a chance to pass him. I'd just pulled out into the passing lane when he swerved toward me. I barely missed getting hit by him."

Storm had gone out at about four in the morning, needing to get out on the open road and clear his head. He was pretty sure the other driver had been returning from a late party.

Melanie sat down on the side of the bed, watching him carefully.

He tried not to wince at the jostling of the bed, but failed.

"Sorry, I'm hurting you."

"Don't worry about it," he responded. "I'm fine." The truth was he didn't want her to leave. He wanted to be close to her.

The delicate touch of her fingertips on his upper arm sent tingles through him. Even his cock stirred a little, which was fucking stupid because he couldn't do anything about it right now.

"Storm, I was so worried about you."

"It's all right. I'm fine." He smiled reassuringly. "At least, I assume I'm fine or I wouldn't be back home. Not fine enough to play a show yet, though, I assume."

"The doctor suggests a couple of weeks of rest." She stroked his cheek with her soft fingers, and the poignancy of her touch, and the deep concern in her eyes, touched him. "Storm, we need to talk."

It was true. They needed to talk about the accident, about the relationship, about where they were going.

But at the insistence of his body, he knew he couldn't start that discussion now. He had to make a trip to the bathroom.

"I know, baby, but not right now." He glanced at her. "I really need to get up."

Reluctantly, she slid from the bed and helped him pull back the covers, then he slowly sat up and placed his feet on the floor.

"Do you want me to help you?" she asked, standing ready beside the bed.

"No, I've got this. Why don't you go make some coffee?"

"Okay, but if you need me, just shout."

She stood for a moment watching him, then finally turned and headed to the door. He knew it was just his pride, but he wanted her to think of him as strong and capable, not see him hobbling around like an old man.

He pushed himself to his feet, then took a tentative step forward. The pain had diminished to an ache and what he was fighting mostly was stiffness in his body. Once he'd gotten to the bathroom and taken care of business, he opened the shower stall and stepped inside. The warm water felt good on his aching muscles. As he relaxed, images flashed through his mind of Melanie coming into the bathroom and stripping off her clothes, then joining him. Another stiffness started in his body and he wrapped his hand around his growing erection and began to pump. He would love to glide into her soft body right now, but the reality was that it would probably be too much for him. But he could manage this, he thought, as he stroked his long, hard cock.

And a part of him needed to. To erase the deep, yet irrational male fear, that the accident might have left him . . . lacking.

A knock sounded on the door. He barely heard it over the sound of the shower. He was pumping with vigor when the door opened.

"Storm, I just wanted to make sure you're okay. Oh . . ." Her gaze fell to his hand wrapped tightly around his swollen cock. "I'm sorry." But instead of leaving, she closed the door behind her and walked toward the shower. She smiled. "Would you like me to help you with that?"

The thought of her stripping down naked and him pounding her against the wall sent hormones surging through him, but in total contradiction, his erection sagged.

He knew it was because he didn't want to look weak in front of her, because he was sure he couldn't manage full-on intercourse with her, yet having a limp cock in his hand didn't really give the impression of a powerful man.

"I'm fine," he said tersely. "I'll be out in a minute."

Melanie's hand gripped the mug tightly as she took a sip of the steaming coffee.

Storm was definitely putting distance between them. Her heart ached as she realized he didn't want her and it was only a matter of time until he admitted it and ended the relationship.

He stepped into the kitchen, wearing the clean clothes she'd set out on the bed—slightly worn jeans and a soft, cotton T-shirt—his hair still damp from his shower. The smell of his woody-musky soap filled her nostrils and she wanted to walk into his arms and be held close to his big body.

"I called Dane," she said.

He walked to the coffeepot and poured himself a cup. "You call him Dane now?" He leaned back against the counter and sipped his coffee black. He smiled. "It's about time."

"I . . . told him that it would be a good idea to arrange to get someone in to help you." She shrugged. "It will be better if you have someone to cook and clean for you for the next little while."

"And you don't want to do that?" He sipped his coffee, watching her face. "I mean, I know I can be a bit of a slob, so I understand."

"Of course, I'd like to do that for you, but . . ." She sucked in a deep breath. "I have the impression that you'd rather not have me around."

His eyebrows arched. "Because I didn't want you to join me in the shower?"

He put down his mug and stepped toward her. "Baby, of course I want you." He reached for her and drew her into his arms and she allowed herself the comfort for a few seconds before she drew away.

"No, not just that. Ever since . . ." She swallowed, not really wanting to bring up that night again. Not wanting to see a look of disgust on his face.

"Ever since what?" he prompted.

She sighed. "Ever since the night we all spent together—you, Travis, Diego, and me—you've been . . . distant."

His lips compressed. "You don't think I'm judging you because of enjoying that night, do you?"

She shrugged. He held her face in his hand and turned it until she looked at him.

"If you remember, I was the one who set that up. Why would I judge you?"

"I don't know. Maybe you assumed I'd turn it down."

"After arranging it with the guys, booking the suite at the out-of-the-way inn, and taking you all the way up there? Why would I do that?"

She shook her head, her eyes shimmering. "I don't know. Maybe you wanted to do it, then afterward, were disgusted by me enjoying it so much."

He flashed her a charming smile and rested his forehead against hers. "You enjoying it was pretty much the point of the whole thing."

She drew back from him, unable to stand the sweet closeness another second. "Then why have you been acting distant to me ever since then? And why did you leave?"

"Ah, fuck. Not because of that. I'm glad you enjoyed it. And it made me fucking hot." His hand stroked over the front of his pants and she glanced down to see a bulge forming under his jeans. "It's making me hot right now just thinking about it."

"Please talk to me, Storm. I want to understand what is happening between us. Whether this relationship has a chance."

"I don't want to talk right now. But I do want to know what would happen if I ordered you to come over here."

She glanced at her fingernails, admiring the black glossy finish, with the metallic red swirls she'd used one of her stamping plates and squishy stamper to apply. "I don't know."

He growled. "Come over here."

She gazed at him. As far as commands went, that was pretty lame. It certainly wasn't enough to override her common sense about fucking him in his state. She smiled. She could go over and stroke him to climax—she was pretty sure that was where this would end up—but not yet.

"I don't think so," she responded.

His lips compressed to a straight line and she could see his enlarged cock straining at the denim.

"I thought you liked following my orders."

She shrugged. "Sure, I like it when you take command, but not today. Maybe later when you haven't just been in a motorcycle accident."

"So what are you trying to do to me?" His gaze glided down her body along the length of her legs.

"I'm trying to help." She stroked a finger along her thigh, drawing the fabric of her blouse up a little. He'd probably be able to see her baby blue lace panties.

"Okay, fine. If you won't come over here, then do this. Sit on the couch with your legs apart."

She smiled and shifted, placing her feet on the floor and widening her legs.

"Good, now pull the crotch of your panties to one side so I can see your pussy."

Her insides trembled as she reached between her thighs and tugged the strip of lace to one side, exposing her intimate folds.

His hand rubbed roughly over the swell in his jeans. "Nice. Now run your finger over yourself and tell me if you're wet."

She stroked her slick flesh. "Yes, very wet."

"Show me."

She held up her finger, shiny from the moisture.

"Come here. I want to suck on your finger."

She smiled and shook her head.

"Fine. Then put it in your mouth and suck it for me."

She slid her finger into her mouth and sucked on it, thinking of his big, hard cock. She stroked it in and out, then sucked until her cheeks hollowed.

"Oh, fuck, I want you, baby."

She sucked harder, continuing to stroke her finger in and out.

"Fuck, get your ass over here now."

Before she realized it she was halfway across the room. Now *that* was an authoritative tone.

"Kneel in front of me and get my fucking cock out."

She knelt down, then stroked over his big bulge. God, he was so thick and hard. She unfastened his snap, then drew the zipper down. Slowly. When she reached inside and wrapped her fingers around him, he groaned.

"God damn it. Suck it, baby."

Barely waiting for him to finish his command, she leaned forward and swallowed his cockhead whole, needing it in her mouth so badly she thought she'd faint. It was hard and filled her mouth so full. She swirled her tongue over the tip, then swallowed the saliva in her mouth, which she'd read caused powerful suction. He groaned so hard, she jerked back.

"Oh, God, did I hurt you?" Damn it, what was she doing? He'd just been in an accident.

He planted his hand on her head and guided her back

to his erection. "Only when you stop. Fuck, that was in-credible."

She laughed and guided his cock between her lips again. She squeezed him in her mouth, then swallowed again, eliciting another groan. She bobbed up and down, taking him deep.

His hand rested on the crown of her head, guiding her to the rhythm he liked.

She could feel him getting close, growing more rigid. "Stop."

At his sudden command, she stopped, then gazed up at him, his cock still deep in her mouth. He grasped her shoulders and drew her upward. His cock fell from her mouth.

"But you were so close."

"I know. But I want to be inside you when I come."

She shook her head. "It's not a good idea."

"It's a fucking excellent idea. Now get up here and get on my cock."

Her hand was still wrapped around his hard, hot member and she wanted it inside her so much, but—

"I said now."

At his sharp command, she found herself stripping off her panties, then kneeling on the couch, straddling him. She grasped his hard cock and guided it to her slick flesh. Slowly, she eased herself down on him, his big cock gliding deep inside her. She whimpered at the sheer pleasure of its girth stretching her tight passage.

Once he was fully immersed in her, they sat eye-to-eye, unmoving. His cock twitched and her muscles tightened in response.

"God damn it, fuck me, woman!"

She gasped at his words and the feel of his pelvis rocking forward, pushing his huge cock a little deeper.

She lifted herself, letting his shaft drag against her inner passage, then she lowered herself. Then lifted again. He grasped her hips and helped her rock up and down. She followed the rhythm he set. He was incredibly hard inside her, and his breathing was rapid.

She was close, intense pleasure pulsing through her, but she fought back the impending orgasm, wanting to wait for him.

She bobbed up and down like a piston, his big member filling her with each stroke. His face was growing red, but he didn't seem to be getting any closer.

She leaned forward and nibbled his ear. "What's wrong, Storm? Am I hurting you?"

"Just keep going." His breathing was hard and there was a note of frustration in his voice.

She took his hand and dragged it inside her blouse, cupping it over her breast. Her hard nipple pushed into his palm. He groaned as he squeezed her soft flesh.

"You feel so fucking good."

She kept riding him, holding back her own pleasure as that big, hard rod filled her again and again.

"That feels incredible, but I want your mouth now," he said, his firm grip on her hips pulling her from his lap, his cock sliding free. "Kneel," he ordered.

She did as she was told, grasping his erection with one hand and stroking it while she cupped his balls with the other. She leaned close and licked one hairless ball, then eased it into her mouth. She licked and caressed it with her tongue. Then she tucked the other into her mouth, too, and stroked and sucked until he groaned.

He grabbed her shoulders. "Fuck, I'm so close. Get on me. Now!"

She shifted to his lap and pushed his cock inside her, then drove down. Immediately, he began to groan. She rode him fast, his cock driving into her deep and hard.

"Oh, fuck. Yeah." He grunted, then she felt hot liquid fill her.

She kept riding him, even as the tension left his body. His cock softened within her and she slowed, then came to rest. She smiled at him and he kissed her. His lips moved tenderly on hers, his arms tightening around her. When their lips parted, she rested her head on his shoulder.

He didn't move, or say anything and she wondered if having her sitting on him like this was painful for him. She drew back, but he pulled her close to his body again, tightening his embrace.

"You didn't come."

"That's okay," she said.

He leaned back and glared at her. "No, it's not okay. This is supposed to be something we both enjoy."

She smiled. "I did enjoy it."

"Great, but you didn't come."

She stroked his whisker-roughened cheek. "I'll come next time."

His hands clenched into fists. "Fuck, you don't get it. If I can't satisfy you . . . if I only satisfy my own hunger . . . what kind of man am I?"

Gazing into his troubled blue eyes, she grasped his face and kissed him.

"You're blowing this way out of proportion. You've just been in an accident." Damn, maybe that wasn't the way to go. Maybe he was afraid something happened in the accident and he wasn't as virile as before.

"I'm not talking about the accident, or whatever temporary effects that might mean," he said. "I'm talking about using your body for my own desires, then leaving you wanting. Only a selfish man does a thing like that."

"A man like your father, you mean?"

He didn't answer, but she could see it in his eyes.

"You are not like your father." She kissed his unreceptive lips, then frowned and drew away. "You never have been and you never will be."

"And yet, every time I go into command mode, I become selfish."

"I don't know where you're getting that." She smiled. "I seem to remember that time in your office, when we pretended I wanted my secretary job back and you ordered me—"

"The first time I took control with Jess, as part of it I punished her. I smacked her as I fucked her, because it helped to get me off . . . but I went too far. I was so concerned about my own pleasure that I hit her again and again, leaving her ass dark red. I hurt her, and I never wanted to do that, but I got caught up in my own selfish

desires. I took what I needed without regard to her pleasure . . . or her pain."

"Oh, Storm. Whatever happened between you and
Jessica, I don't believe that you were selfish. And I'm sure
Jessica wouldn't have allowed it to go further than she
wanted it to." She stroked his raspy cheek and gazed into
his eyes. "And I know you didn't hurt me." She kissed
him. "There's nothing wrong with getting caught up in
your own pleasure. It takes two, you know. I could have
changed things to be more conducive to my own pleasure,
but this time I was more concerned about you. You've
been in an accident. You're stressed and you were having
problems. I wanted to ensure it worked for you."

"It doesn't mean—"

She kissed his lips, stopping the words.

"Look, I held back. I could barely stop the orgasm
you were giving me, but with great strength of will"—
she grinned and nuzzled his neck—"I was able to do it. I
held back that storm of pleasure, and I'm quite proud of
myself." She pursed her lips. "Don't take that away from
me."

Storm stared into her glittering eyes, her pursed lips hiding her smile.

God, this woman was more than he deserved.

"So you're saying you were able to resist the dizzying
effect of my huge cock driving into you again and again?"

She smiled and nodded.

"You're right, that is quite an accomplishment." He
grinned and his hand stroked down her stomach, then

between her legs. "I guess that means you're still turned on. And very close."

"Yes, but don't you think you should—oh!"

His fingers had found her slick flesh and slid inside her. She grasped his shoulders, her fingers curling around him.

He stroked her clit and she moaned.

"I really think you should—"

"Silence."

At his commanding tone, her eyes widened and her mouth closed.

"Now sit on the couch and spread your legs. I want to see that slick pussy of yours."

She slid from his lap and opened her legs. Her folds glistened in the light.

He pushed himself from the couch to the floor, hiding the effects of the painful transition. It hurt to move, but he didn't want her to see that. He leaned forward, ignoring the complaints of his body and stroked her thighs, then buried his face in her slick flesh. He drove his tongue into her soft, wet opening, swirling in a rapid spiral. Her moans of pleasure gave him deep satisfaction.

His finger found her clit and he stroked it. She grasped his shoulders. His fingers glided the length of her slit and he found her clit with his tongue. As he flicked it, he simultaneously drove two fingers inside her. She gasped.

"Do you like that?" he asked as he finger-fucked her.

"Oh, yes."

He licked her clit again, keeping a steady rhythm going with his fingers.

"Tell me when you come."

He covered her with his mouth again and licked and then began to suck on the small button. She arched against him, moaning. His fingers drove deep into her hot, silky depths and he could feel his cock growing hard again. She moaned, then her fingers tightened around his shoulders.

"Oh, God, yes. I'm going to—"

He sucked hard on her clit.

She arched again. "Oh, I'm coming." She wailed, that sweet sound of release he loved to hear so much.

He kept driving into her and sucking while she rode the wave of pleasure, gasping for air, then wailing again. Long and loud.

Finally, she collapsed against the couch and he slowed, then drew back from her sweet, wet pussy.

She gazed at him, her eyes warm and full of love.

"You see? You had nothing to worry about," he said.

She laughed. "You're right. I never should have doubted you."

Storm sat in an easy chair reading, wondering where Melanie had gone. She'd finished the breakfast dishes a while ago, then disappeared down the hall. He had hoped she'd come and curl up beside him and they could read together, or talk, though talking would probably lead to a discussion about their relationship and he wasn't sure he was ready for that yet. He was still annoyed with himself for putting his needs above hers, even though she'd de-fused the discussion with her adorable and loving manner. He still felt he should have put her pleasure first, or at least made it as high a priority as his own.

Melanie walked down the hallway carrying a small plastic bin. "Do you need anything?" she asked, poised at the doorway to the kitchen.

"Maybe a coffee," he said.

She smiled and headed into the kitchen, then returned a moment later and handed him a steaming cup.

"Are you going to join me?" he asked.

"Actually, I was going into the kitchen to do my nails."

"Why don't you do them here?"

She bit her lower lip. "I wouldn't want to chance getting polish on your carpet, and it has a strong odor."

He raised an eyebrow. "Do you usually spill your polish?"

"No, but accidents do happen."

He shrugged. "Don't worry about it. Bring your stuff out here."

"What about the smell?"

"I don't care about any of that." He smiled. "I just like being with you."

She smiled as she turned around, then retrieved the bin from the kitchen. She sat cross-legged on the floor in front of the glass coffee table, facing him. She laid down several layers of paper towels, then opened the bin and set out several bottles of polish, some clear, a couple of dark colors, and a couple of translucent creamy colors with shimmery flakes floating in them. After she finished painting a clear base coat on her nails, she examined the dark colors.

She glanced up to see him watching her. She lifted two of the bottles. "Do you like the green or the purple better?"

"They both look black to me."

"This is a blackened purple and this is a hunter green."

He shrugged. "I can't really tell, but I like green."

She smiled. "Okay. Green it is."

After she'd applied the polish, she picked up one of the creams and turned it upside down, then rolled it between her hands. She opened the bottle and as she stroked the brush over the surface of her nail, he was amazed to see shimmery, opalescent green flakes appear.

"That's pretty impressive," he commented.

She grinned. "I love flakies. They're so easy to do, yet the result is always stunning."

She then proceeded to apply a clear coat of polish over the shimmery green nails.

A buzzing sounded and she glanced at her cell on the table next to her.

"I just got a text from Travis," she said. "He wants to know if he can FaceTime you."

Storm grabbed his tablet from the side table. "I'll answer him." He opened the app and clicked on Travis's e-mail. A moment later, Travis's smiling face showed up on the screen.

"Hey, man. You still lazing around while the rest of us are working hard?"

Storm shrugged. "You bet."

Diego's face appeared beside Travis's. "Hey, man. How you doing?"

The view on the tablet shifted until the faces of all four band members were staring at him. He chatted with them for a while, Melanie joining in. The guys expressed their concern and best wishes for him to return to them quickly. He loved talking to them, but he couldn't help remembering the night he'd shared Melanie with Travis and Diego.

Melanie laughed at something Diego said, then Travis teased her about something. Storm remembered Travis commanding Melanie to go down on Storm that night, and his cock swelled at the memory. Suddenly, all he could think of was how Melanie had called Travis master, and how she'd bowed to his every command.

His cock ached with need and he had to fight the urgent desire to end the call and demand she drop in front of him and bring him to release. At that moment, there was nothing he wanted more than to hear her call *him* master.

"Storm?"

He glanced up to see Melanie gazing at him in concern.

"Are you okay?" she asked.

"Sure."

Melanie gazed at the screen. "We should be going. I hope the show goes well tonight."

They all said their good-byes and she closed the app.

The temptation to command her to kneel in front of him and take out his aching cock, rocked through him, becoming almost unbearable. He knew she would willingly obey him. In fact, judging from the past, her pussy would be dripping before her knees touched the carpet. He could imagine what it would feel like to stroke her and feel the slickness of her flesh.

But he resisted the temptation to command her, still reluctant to take that path, despite his intense desire to bend her to his will. It was the sheer intensity of his desire that unnerved him now. A need he wasn't sure he could control.

She hesitated, as if she sensed his internal struggle, but finally she stood up. "I'll just go clean up this mess."

She swept up her polishes and other paraphernalia and put them in the bin, then balled up the paper towels and carried it all into the kitchen.

His cell buzzed and he picked it up, happy for the distraction.

"Yeah."

"It's Dane. Are you up for visitors? We were just out for lunch, so we're close by."

"Sure. Come on up."

Melanie returned a few minutes later. "Who were you talking to?"

"Dane. He and Jess will be here in a few minutes."

"I'll go put some fresh coffee on. I know Dane usually likes one this time of day."

She still stumbled a little over using Dane's first name. She headed into the kitchen. When the knock sounded on the door a few minutes later, however, she hurried to the door to answer it.

"Hi, Melanie." Jessica gave her a big hug.

Dane headed into the living room and Melanie and Jessica followed.

"I'll get some coffee," Melanie said.

"No, don't bother," Jessica said as Dane headed toward the kitchen. "I'm just going to have a short visit with Rafe, then I want you to join me for some shopping."

"Thanks for the invitation, but I'd rather just stay here."

"Nonsense. You can use some time away from the apartment." Jessica smiled. "And I happened across a new boutique a few streets over that carries nail polishes from that new indie brand you told me about."

"You mean Shine?"

Jessica nodded. "And they've got cute nail accessories, too. Little rhinestone bows, studs, gemstones, micro beads. I'm dying to see what you'd do with half the stuff."

Melanie bit her lip and Storm knew she didn't want to leave him, but the temptation Jessica offered was calling to her.

Dane returned with a mug of coffee in his hand. He sat in the armchair kitty-corner to Storm.

"Go ahead, Melanie. It'll give Dane and me a chance to talk," Storm said.

"And Dane promised not to talk about work," Jessica said, "so no worries there."

"Okay, I'll just go change."

As Melanie disappeared down the hall, Jessica sat beside Storm and gave him a hug, then took his hand. "So are you doing okay?"

"I'm fine."

"We were so worried about you." She stared at him with her big green eyes.

He gazed at her with warmth. He had once believed he was in love with Jessica, and had been heartbroken when she had turned down his marriage proposal, but he knew now that it hadn't been that kind of love between them. But she would always be precious to him because she had been the first to love him for who he was. The first to make him feel truly special. And now, she was even more precious because she made his brother so happy.

"I know," he said, "but I really am fine."

Melanie returned and Jessica stood up. "Okay, we'll be back in about an hour."

He watched them disappear out the door.

"So what happened?" Dane asked.

Storm gazed at his brother. "You mean the accident?"

Dane nodded.

"I swerved to miss a deer."

"Why were you out on the bike?"

Storm shrugged. "I was out for a ride. What's the big deal?"

Dane's lips compressed. "I may not know Storm as well as I know Rafe, but I do know that mornings have never been your thing. When you were younger, and something was bothering you, you'd have trouble sleeping and would wind up rising early and going out for a ride on your bike, or going for a long walk." Dane placed his coffee mug on the table. "I just think you had something on your mind that day and might want to talk it out." He sat back. "Are you worried about telling me you want to stay in the band?"

"You already know that."

"True. And I encouraged you to go back on tour."

This was his brother's way of fishing for information.

"Then is it something about Melanie?" Dane asked.

Storm wasn't really comfortable discussing his issues with his brother. But he realized his brother was probably the only one who might come close to understanding.

"It's clear that she is in love with you," Dane went on. "And it's become increasingly clear, to me anyway, that you feel the same way. I doubt she knows it, though." He arched an eyebrow. "Unless you've told her."

Part of Storm wanted to tell Dane to mind his own business, but deep inside he was touched and pleased that his brother was reaching out to him and wanted to help. And right now Storm could use the help.

"No, I haven't."

"Does it have anything to do with your past relationship with Jessica?"

Storm shook his head. "At first maybe. But we're way past that."

"So what's holding you back?"

"It's not Melanie. She's incredible."

Dane smiled and nodded. "What is it then?"

Storm leaned back and raked his hand through his hair. "Ah, fuck, it's me. It's what I want. Or what I shouldn't want."

"And what is that?"

Storm shrugged and stared at his coffee cup. "The way you are with Jessica. The way you . . . control her in the bedroom. That . . . appeals to me."

Dane shrugged. "And how does Melanie feel about that?"

Storm raked his hand through his hair again. "I shouldn't be telling you personal things about Melanie."

Dane leaned forward. "I'm not going to tell anyone. Not even Jessica. And if it will help your relationship . . ."

Storm nodded. "Fine. She loves it when I take control."

"Great, then what's the problem?"

"Ah, fuck. You know what Dad was like." Pain lanced through Storm at the memory of the cruelties he'd suffered at his father's hand. Being smacked across the room by a vicious blow when he was only six years old. Being beaten by his father's belt so hard he had painful, bleeding welts. And his father seemed to enjoy inflicting the pain.

"You didn't like it when I punished Jessica that night," Dane said. "But you also knew how much it turned her on. And you know I didn't hurt her. It was nothing like what our father did to you."

Storm's hands clenched into fists. "But when I punished her . . ." His throat closed up and he felt like he was going to choke. He sucked in air, calming himself. "I went too far. I *hurt* her."

"Storm, let me tell you something."

The fact his brother called him Storm didn't slip past his notice. That acceptance by his brother warmed his heart.

"I saw what happened that night. I woke up when I felt Jessica slip from the bed to go find you and I followed. I didn't mean to spy, but she was reaching out to you and"—he shrugged—"I wanted to see if she succeeded."

"So you saw what I did to her."

"I saw that you'd had a bit to drink and you got a little carried away, took her a little roughly. But it was no big deal. If Jessica had been in any real distress, she would have stopped you, or called out for help." Dane's gaze locked with Storm's. "And the same with Melanie. She'll let you know if she doesn't like what you're doing."

"She shouldn't have to."

Dane smiled. "Right. Because you have to get it perfect every time." He leaned back in the chair. "Don't worry. You'll get to know what she likes, how much, how far you can go. It's part of being in a relationship. Getting to know what works in the bedroom."

Storm stared at him doubtfully. "But what if I don't know my own limits? What if I lose control and . . . lash out at her? What if I cross the line into violence?"

"You won't. That's not the kind of man you are. And she's not a scared, powerless child being beaten by a cruel adult." He paused, watching Storm carefully. "You're not our father. You have never been, nor will you ever be, like him."

Storm compressed his lips. "That's what Melanie said."

Dane smiled. "There are so many reasons I like that woman." He tipped his head. "So? Do you believe her?"

At Storm's hesitation, Dane asked, "Do you really think you'd ever hurt Melanie?"

Storm stared at his brother, and knew deep in his heart that the answer was no.

Melanie finished emptying the dishwasher while Jessica set the tray of used glasses from the living room on the counter. Jessica and Dane had joined them for dinner, then they'd watched a movie afterward.

As soon as Jessica and Dane left, Melanie went to the master bedroom and fetched her backpack. She'd spent last night sleeping in the armchair by Storm's bed, to ensure she was there if he needed anything, but tonight she planned to sleep in the guest room so she could get some sleep. She appeared in the living room and set down the bag.

"I've laid your pajamas on the bed and put your pain-killers and a glass of water on the side table." She wanted to ask if he needed help getting ready for bed, but she didn't want to hurt his male pride. She knew he wouldn't want to depend on her. "Do you need anything else?"

He stood up. Slowly, clearly still in some pain.

"No, thanks. Just looking forward to getting into bed."

"Okay, good night then." She picked up her pack.

"What's going on?"

"I'm going to sleep in the guest room."

"Why the hell would you do that?"

She hesitated. "I could sleep in the chair again."

"Or in the bed."

"I don't think that's a good idea. You're still in pain.

If I move around in the night, it will disturb you. You need a good night's sleep."

"What I need is you in bed with me. And I fully plan on having you *move around*."

She stood frozen, her hand still gripping her pack tightly, unsure of what to do. Standing there staring at her, he looked as imposing as ever. Strong and virile. She longed to race forward and throw herself into his muscular, tattooed arms. But she had to be realistic.

"I'm sorry. I think it's better this way." She turned and walked toward the other bedroom.

"Freeze."

At his commanding tone, a tremor of excitement rippled down her spine, and she stopped midstride.

"Turn around."

She turned to face him.

"I want you in my bed tonight, so that's where you'll go."

She gazed at him uncertainly. His blue gaze bore through her.

"Now," he snapped.

She surged forward, her insides tingling, and scampered down the hall to his room. He followed her, moving slowly but purposefully. She turned and waited, setting down her pack while he entered the room.

"Strip."

She sucked in a breath and pulled up the hem of her shirt, then pulled the garment over her head and tossed it aside. His heated gaze settled on her lace-clad breasts as she unfastened the button on her jeans, then drew the zipper down. She shed the pants, and her socks, then stood before him in only skimpy purple lace panties and matching bra.

His eyebrows quirked up. "I didn't say to stop."

She reached behind and unfastened her bra, intensely aware of his hot gaze on her breasts. She released the hooks and slid the bra from her shoulders and dropped it to the floor. He stared at her nipples and they hardened to tight buds. She hooked her thumbs under the elastic of her panties and pushed them down her legs, then kicked them aside.

Now she stood before him, totally naked.

It was like being stroked by hot silk as his frank masculine gaze slid the length of her, from top to toe, then back up to settle on her shaven mound. She found it hard to breathe under his scrutiny.

He took a step toward her, then another. Her breath held as he grew closer. So close she could feel the heat of his body. Then he stepped past her and walked toward the cozy chair at the end of the bed. He turned it to face the bed, and pushed it closer, until it was only about a foot away, then sat down.

"Get on the bed, facing the headboard, on your hands and knees."

She obeyed, climbing onto the satiny, fine cotton duvet cover, facing away from him.

"Drop your head to the bed, then reach around behind and open yourself to me."

Her heart thumped loudly as she rested her cheek on

the bed and reached around to grasp her buttocks to open her flesh to him. God, she wanted him to touch her.

Storm stared at her feminine folds, displayed openly to him with her hands gripping each side of her ass. He simply stared, saying nothing, and could see her opening growing moist, proving how much this turned her on.

"Do you like me looking at you?" he asked.

She squirmed a little but answered quietly, "Yes."

"Would you like me to touch you?" he asked.

"Yes."

The need in her voice made him smile.

"Good. But right now I would like you to touch that dripping wet pussy of yours."

She released her ass and slid one hand to her stomach, then between her legs. He watched raptly as her fingers found her slick folds and stroked the length of them.

"Show me how you'd like me to touch you."

She stroked back and forth, then her fingers dipped inside. She thrust lightly a couple of times, then slid out and stroked over her clit.

But despite how open she was to him, he couldn't see as much as he'd like.

"Lie on your back."

Her fingers slipped away from her intimate flesh and she rolled over and laid down, close to the end of the bed, with her knees bent.

"Now continue."

Her fingers found her folds again and she stroked their slick length, then her fingertip moved to her clit.

"Show me how you make yourself come."

She opened the fleshy folds, exposing the button, then her fingertip quivered over it. He could hear her breathing accelerate as she stroked and teased her clit.

His cock ached and he unzipped and freed it from its confines, wrapping his hand around the hard shaft.

"Does it feel good?" he asked.

"Oh, yes."

He stroked his cock.

"Call me Master."

"Yes, Master."

He almost groaned at the words. Here she was, her legs splayed wide in front of him, touching herself for his pleasure, willing to do anything he commanded.

Why the fuck had it taken him so long to realize that this was a good thing?

Her fingers rippled over her wet flesh.

"Are you getting close?" he asked.

"Oh yes, Master."

"Do you want to come?"

"Yes." Her voice trembled with need.

"Good. Now stop."

She whimpered as she drew her hand away.

"Get back on your hands and knees and show me your ass," he said sharply. "You need to be punished."

She changed positions quickly, thrusting her naked ass into the air. "But, why, Master?"

"Let's get something straight right now. As your Master, I can punish you at any time, any way I want, for any reason I want. Understand?"

"Yes, Master. You can punish me anytime you like, even if I didn't do anything wrong."

He smiled at her words and stroked her delightfully round ass. "So you're being a smart ass." He stood up and drew back his hand and smacked her ass sharply. She let out a small gasp of surprise.

"When I tell you to do something, you do it with pleasure, even if you want to do something different, do you understand? As my slave, you should be happy for my guidance."

"Oh, yes, I am, Master."

"All right." He stroked her slightly red ass, then dragged his fingertips over her slick folds to reward her. She moaned softly.

He stroked her ass again and smacked, then immediately stroked her folds. After the next smack, he dipped his fingers inside her slick opening and swirled, then withdrew.

"Do you like your punishment?"

She squirmed under his hand as he stroked her ass. "Oh, yes, Master. Thank you."

He chuckled, then smacked again. He glided two fingers inside her and began to stroke in and out, then smacked again, his fingers still moving inside her. He pushed his fingers deep, then found her clit with his thumb and teased it while he smacked her again.

"Oh, yes." She arched her back, thrusting her ass higher.

He thrust his fingers inside her several times, then smacked again. He pushed his fingers deep, then rippled his thumb over her button. She moaned.

"You want to come?" he murmured.

"Yes, Master. Please let me come."

He smacked her ass a little harder. It was a rosy red now.

"I want to hear you come as I smack your pert little ass." He thrust his fingers deep, again and again, as he continued to smack with the other hand.

Melanie's ass burned as pleasure spiked through her. The pleasure and pain he was giving her merged into a raw, incredibly intense set of sensations that drove her closer to the edge. She gasped and arched, then moaned. She wanted to feel the flat of his hand connect with her flesh as his fingers drove into her sensitive, inner passage.

His thumb quivered over her clit, then his palm smacked across her ass.

"Oh, yes. Oh, God, yes." The intensity of the pleasure blasting through her sent her sailing to heaven. She wailed, long and loud, as an orgasm blasted through her.

Even before the pleasure subsided, she felt the blunt tip of his cock brush against her folds, then he pressed forward. His cock drove inside and filled her to the hilt.

"Oh, yes." She nearly fainted from the incredible feel of his big shaft driving into her.

"Oh, fuck, you feel so good." He drew back, then thrust forward again.

Her pleasure skyrocketed as his big cock filled her again and again, driving deep and hard each time. She squeezed him tightly within her and he groaned.

"Fuck." His hand pushed under her belly and he lifted her hips, then his other hand glided down her stomach. The instant he found her clit, she moaned. He flicked over it and she gasped, then plunged over the edge again. He kept thrusting and a moment later, he ground against her, groaning. She felt his hot seed release inside her, filling her with heat.

He groaned again and rolled to his side, taking her with him. They lay there, spooned together, his cock still inside her.

She wiggled her ass against him, squeezing his limp cock inside her. He groaned and she realized it might be in pain, not pleasure. She'd totally forgotten about his accident. She rolled around to face him. He was still in his T-shirt and boxers, having shed his jeans somewhere along the way.

"Are you okay?" She stroked his hair from his forehead.

"Of course. Better than okay."

But his voice was strained.

"Okay, time for some tender, loving care." She pushed herself to her feet. "Wait here."

She hurried into the bathroom and started the water in the big tub, then returned. Storm had moved back to the chair, so she stepped behind him and massaged his shoulders and his upper back, feeling the tense bundles of muscles under his skin.

"Do you want a painkiller?" she asked.

"No, just keep doing what you're doing."

She smiled as she continued to run her hands along his muscular back and shoulders, enjoying his murmurs of approval.

"I think it's time for a nice hot bath." She walked around the chair and held out her hand to him. His gaze slid the length of her naked body and he smiled.

"With you like that, I'll follow you anywhere." He stood up and took her hand.

Inside the large, marble-floored bathroom, she grabbed the hem of his T-shirt and pushed it up. He tugged it over his head and discarded it. She curled her fingers under the waistband of his boxers and lowered them, coming face-to-face with his semi-erect cock. She laughed and kissed it, then stood up and turned off the flow of water into the tub.

"You go in first," she said.

"So you're joining me." He climbed in and settled into the warm water.

"Of course." She smiled. "How does the water feel?"

He leaned back. "Wonderful."

She climbed in, and settled on the opposite side of the large oval tub, facing him.

"You know, you're entirely too far away." He held out his hand to her.

She took it and pulled herself forward. He stretched his legs out and she straddled his thighs.

"I thought you were done."

"But here I'm relaxed and you can do all the work."

She laughed. "That's true." She glided forward until

her sensitive folds rested against the base of his growing cock. She wrapped her arms around him, pressed her body to his, and kissed him. He slid his arms around her and his tongue delved into her as he returned her kiss with passion. She rocked against his cock as the kiss deepened. He grew bigger and harder and her flesh ached to have him inside her again.

Their lips parted and he stared deeply into her eyes.

"I love you, Melanie."

She stared into his sky blue eyes, simmering with heat, but she knew his words had nothing to do with lust.

Tears welled in her eyes. "I love you, too."

She pressed her hand between their stomachs and grasped his rock-hard cock, then lifted her body. With their gazes still locked, she glided down on it. She watched the sparks flash in his eyes as she took him deep.

She kissed him, pressing her tongue into his warm mouth.

He drew back, gazing into her eyes. "I really, really love you."

At his words, her heart swelled.

He took her hand and pressed his lips to her dark green fingernails adorned with iridescent flakes. "From your artistically painted fingernails to your bluebird tattoo"—his finger stroked over the tattoo on her breast—"to your rosy little ass. I will do whatever makes you happy." He caught her gaze again. "And be my true self in the process."

She kissed his nose and grinned. "Which I assume includes being a bossy master in the bedroom."

He laughed. "Or the living room, or the kitchen, or the office."

"The office? So you're going back to work at Ranier Industries?"

"Occasionally. When I have time between tours with the band. But when I do go into the office, I'm looking forward to dealing with my secretary. I'm sure she'll need to be kept in line."

The memory of him pushing her against the wall and holding her hands pinned over her head made heat burn through her.

"I'm sure she will," she said in a throaty voice. She squeezed his big cock inside her and he groaned.

She laughed and nuzzled his neck, feeling his cock twitch inside her.

"Right now, I think you need some special therapy." She drew back, then glided the length of his cock again. He was thick and hard inside her. Stroking her passage as she drew back again.

She drove down. His hands grasped her hips, stopping her before she could glide away again.

"Wait. I need to ask you something," he said.

"What is it?"

"It really should be me on my knees instead of you."

Her heart skipped a beat.

"Melanie, I love you. I want to be with you always."

Her insides trembled as she stared deeply into his beloved eyes.

"Will you marry me?" he asked.

She drew in a deep breath of pure joy, then squeezed

him mercilessly. He groaned and she cupped his cheeks and kissed him, driving her tongue deep into his mouth.

"Yes."

He shifted his pelvis, pushing his cock deeper into her.

"Oh, God, yes."

He kissed her again and rocked into her. She began moving, gliding up and down his shaft, taking it deep each time. Pleasure built in her, higher and higher, as he moaned with her steady strokes. The warm water surged around them as she thrust again and again, moving on him in a steady rhythm, driving her pleasure higher and higher.

"Fuck, woman," he said between breaths. "I'm going to explode any second."

She laughed and bounced faster, squeezing him as she moved.

"Fuck, ohhhh . . ."

She felt liquid heat explode within her and she gasped. His thumb brushed her clit and her world shattered. She wailed as she shot straight to ecstasy.

Finally, she slumped against him, her head resting on his shoulder.

After a few moments, she shifted, then nuzzled his neck. "I take it you've finally come to the realization that you are nothing like your father."

"I finally came to realize that what we do is totally different. When I punish you, it is as much for your pleasure as for mine. It is only because you enjoy it that it turns me on." He squeezed her shoulders. "And I know you're strong. If I ever made a mistake, and pushed too far, you would let me know."

She smiled and kissed him again. "Yes, I would. But I'm sure that would never happen." She stroked his shoulders. "I love it when you take control, and I know you would only do what brings us both pleasure."

He took her in his arms again and kissed her tenderly. "I really love you."

She stroked his hair from his face, her lips turning up in a broad smile. "I'm so happy right now."

She snuggled against him again, and gazed up at him.

"So I'm going to be married to a rock star slash billionaire CEO slash Dominant?"

"That's right. Do you have a problem with that?" he asked, eyebrow arched upward.

She laughed. "Absolutely not."

In fact, it sounded like heaven on earth.

Epilogue

Melanie held Storm's hand as they walked along the stone path leading away from the huge Ranier country home. This was where Dane and Jessica were going to be married. The four of them were going to spend the weekend here to discuss plans for the upcoming wedding. It would also allow Dane and Storm to spend some brotherly time together, and for Melanie and Jessica to catch up.

Storm and Melanie had arrived a day early so Storm could show her around the impressive vacation home where he'd spent many happy summers. Shortly after they'd arrived and dropped their stuff off in the luxurious private suite in the huge house, Storm had insisted they go out and see the lake. He was like a little boy on his first day of summer vacation.

"I want to show you my favorite place in the world," Storm said as they walked toward the glittering lake. "I had some of the best times of my life as a kid when our parents brought us here in the summer. A big reason was because our father joined us only on the weekends."

Jessica squeezed his hand, knowing he must be thinking about the abusive times in the past with his father.

"But him not being here was only part of it," Storm continued. "It was a time when Dane and I could just be little boys. We could actually forget about performing for our father and being perfect little Ranier men, and just be ourselves. It's looking back on those times now that I realize that Dane had it just as bad as me. He didn't have the physical beatings, but he had to be who Dad wanted him to be because that's just how Dane is made."

They walked past a stand of trees toward the water. They stepped from the stone path onto the grass, then toward a narrow sandy beach and a comfortable-looking park bench overlooking the water.

"You're saying that he had to follow the rules someone else set for him," Melanie said. "That seems so strange because he doesn't answer to anyone now."

"That's right. His survival technique was to be the one who made the rules. And to me, that looked like he had become our father, but now I know he just wanted to become himself. Just like I did. But Dane has compassion and understanding. He proved *that* when he took my ideas for the business and implemented them. In a way, I was being like our father to him by being disappointed in how he ran the company before he even got started."

They slowed as they approached the bench and she squeezed his hand again. "But he understood. He knew how much you needed to get away from that world. And now you've found a balance."

He stopped and pulled her into his arms, a smile on his face. "I found that balance thanks to you."

He kissed her, deeply and passionately, causing her toes to curl. She knew she would never get tired of feeling his big hard body against her, and his big protective arms around her.

His compelling blue eyes gazed deeply into hers. "If it weren't for you, I'd still be sitting in that corporate world instead of doing what I truly love: traveling with the band and performing in front of enthusiastic fans."

She grinned. "You mean ones who flash their boobs at you?"

He grinned. "Yes, there are many perks to my job." His hand slid up her side and he cupped her breast. "I have sexy groupies try to entice me into their beds." His fingers caressed her, until her nipple blossomed into a hard nub, sending heat tingling through her. "And there's this one that my drummer and the lead guitarist even share with me." He pinched her aching nipple. "That's pretty hot."

"As I recall," she said, her voice a little breathless as he began to stroke her other breast, "you only did that once and it shook you up a little."

He chuckled. "Yeah, well I wasn't as sure of myself back then." He nuzzled her neck. "But that was so hot, I might see that happening again."

She smiled impishly. "But what if the groupie doesn't want to."

"Ha!" He turned her around, still holding her close to his body and his hands covered both her breasts, caressing them firmly, his thumbs teasing her hard nipples, sending electric thrills through her. "I happen to know this groupie will do anything I tell her." He slid one hand down her belly, then slipped the tips of his fingers under her jeans, sending her pulse skyrocketing. "Isn't that right?"

When she said nothing, still trying to catch her breath, he slid deeper, his fingers gliding under her panties and one dipping into her slick folds.

"Isn't that right?" he murmured again, against her ear.

"Yes, sir." The words came out hoarse and breathy as his fingers stroked her, then she gasped as his fingertip brushed her clit.

He laughed and drew his hand from under the denim. He gazed out over the water where she assumed little Rafe and Dane had gone swimming together as children.

"When I was a teenager, I always dreamed of going skinny-dipping here with a girl." He pointed toward the lake. "See the big rock out there?"

She nodded at the sight of a large rock pushing about a half foot from the water, the exposed surface big enough to sit on.

"We used to swim out there as kids. When I got older, and taller," he grinned, "I found the water only reached my chest. In fact, I realized that it was the perfect place to . . . oh, let's say get traction."

"You mean if a couple wanted to get down and dirty in the water?"

"That's right." He turned her around to face him again and pressed her an arm's length from him. "Now take off your clothes," he commanded.

Her breath caught. Storm had been practicing his newly found dominant abilities with breathlessly exciting results. When he used that firm authoritative tone with her, she melted.

She stripped off her shirt, dropping it to the grass, then unfastened her jeans and let them fall to the ground. She stepped out of them, shivering in excitement at what was to come. Thank God they had come to the house a day early, so there was no one else around, because she was sure even if the house had been teeming with people who might spy them out by the lake, she still would have stripped just as quickly if he commanded it.

He watched intently as she unfastened her bra. When she pulled it from her body, his hot gaze brushed across her nipples like a physical caress. She pushed down her tiny panties and pulled them off, then handed them to him as he liked her to do.

He smiled and shoved them into the pocket of his jeans.

"Sit down on the bench."

She sat down on the wooden surface, the smooth wood cool against her skin.

He knelt in front of her. "I want to lick you. Where would you like me to do that?"

She knew exactly where she wanted him to lick her, but she didn't want to say, "Down there."

At her hesitation, he grinned. "Baby, I want to hear

you talk dirty. I want to hear you use those dirty words you wouldn't ordinarily say."

She nodded, but still couldn't quite bring herself to say certain words, so she said, "I want you to lick my breasts."

He chuckled. "You can do better than that." He stroked over one hard nipple and said, "Repeat after me. 'I want you to squeeze my tits.'"

A quiver fluttered down her spine. "I want you to squeeze my tits," she repeated obediently.

He stroked her breasts, then squeezed lightly, his thumbs dabbing at her hard nipples.

"Now say 'I want you to suck my tits.'"

"I want you to suck my tits," she repeated, stumbling a little over the last word.

He leaned forward and covered one hard, aching nipple with his mouth and drew deeply. She sucked in a breath at the exquisite pleasure.

"Now what would you like me to do?" he asked, eyebrow raised.

"I want you to . . . uh . . ." she was wet and slick between her legs and wanted him there.

He chuckled. "Say 'I want you to lick my cunt.'"

She bit her lower lip. "I don't really like that word." But she knew she'd say it if he commanded it.

He nuzzled her neck. "Because it makes you feel dirty, right?"

She gazed at him and nodded.

"Okay, then say 'I want you to lick my pussy.'"

"I . . ." Her cheeks flushed. "I want you to lick my pussy."

He grinned broadly. "Very good." He stood up and took her hand, then drew her to her feet, too.

"But . . . I thought you were going to . . . ah . . ."

He laughed. "Still need a little work, I see." He kissed her lightly. "I rather like this repeat-after-me game."

He sat down on the bench. "Kneel in front of me."

She knelt on the grass in front of him.

"Say 'I want to . . .'"

"I want to . . ."

"'. . . feel your big cockhead . . .'"

Her gaze dropped to the bulge forming under his jeans. ". . . feel your big cockhead . . ."

"'. . . in my mouth as I suck you.'"

He took her hand and placed it on his hard erection. Then he guided her to unzip the pants. She reached into his pants and wrapped her fingers around the thick base of his shaft.

". . . in my mouth as I suck you." She drew out his big cock and wrapped her lips around him, then sucked.

"Oh, fuck." He groaned and cupped her head, then stilled it as she started to move on him. "Now say 'I want to . . .'"

She drew away from him, smiling at the effect she had on him. "I want to . . ."

"'Feel your huge cock drive deep into me . . .'"

"Feel your huge cock drive deep into me . . ." she repeated. And, God, she ached for him to do that.

"'While you fuck me hard against the rock.'"

Oh, yeah.

"While you fuck me hard against the rock." The words came out a little breathless and her hold tightened on his cock.

To her surprise, he grasped her wrist and drew her hand away.

"Now say 'I want to . . .'"

"I want to . . ." Anticipation shot through her. She couldn't wait for him to drive into her, but would play this game as long as he wanted her to.

"'. . . ask you to . . .'" he said his eyes glowing.

". . . ask you to . . ." She smiled.

"'. . . marry me.'"

". . . marry me," she repeated automatically before the words fully registered. Then her eyes widened as she realized what she'd just said.

"I . . . but . . ." she stammered.

His lips turned up in a grin. "So ask me, then."

"I . . . don't understand." Had he just proposed?

He took her hand and kissed it. "I proposed to a woman once, down on my knees, and it did not go well." He shrugged. "I thought this time, I'd turn it around."

She gazed into his intent blue eyes and realized he really did want her to ask him.

Her heart swelled. She wanted to ask him. Because she wanted to be with him forever.

She took his hand and pressed it to her chest, gazing at him solemnly. "Storm, feel my heart beating. It's pounding because I want you. Every time we're together I'm filled with need and intense desire. That's because I want you so much. In every way. Not just in my bed. But in my life. You are my hero in everything you do, and I know that with your help I am growing into who I truly want to be."

She raised his hand to her lips and kissed his palm, then entwined her fingers with his. "Please, Storm. Will you marry me?"

He laughed joyfully, then pulled her into his arms and kissed her, his lips moving with passion. Then suddenly, he bent down and threw her over his shoulder and stood up. Still fully dressed he waded into the water, his hand stroking her behind.

She laughed at the craziness of it all. "You haven't answered me, Storm."

As he continued to walk, his fingers glided along her exposed slit, sending sparks through her.

"I know. Be patient, my love." Then he glided a finger inside her and she sucked in air.

He slowed and she found herself tipped back, then she was sitting on that big rock he'd pointed out earlier. It pressed against her aching folds. She squirmed a little.

Storm laughed again and spread her knees wide.

"I want to lick you. Where would you like me to do that?"

Her lips turned up in a grin. This time she wouldn't let him distract her. "I want you to lick my pussy." She felt strange saying that word, but using it made her feel wicked and sexy. Really bad-ass, like a biker, rocker chick should be.

Storm laughed and drove his tongue into her. It swirled in her passage, then his finger slipped inside her and he licked upward, then fluttered the tip of his tongue against her clit. She clung to his head, holding him against her.

"Fuck, I want you so bad," he said as he pulled her forward. She sank into the water, her back gliding along the flat, vertical wall of the rock. When she was deep enough, she felt Storm's hard cockhead press against her, then he drove inside her, crushing her to the rock. She wrapped her legs around his body and he pushed deeper still. For a moment, they just stood there, him fully immersed in her, in a timeless moment of pure intimacy.

Then he drew back and drove forward again.

"You asked me a question a few minutes ago," he said.

God, he was right. How had she almost forgotten? Then he pulled back and drove into her again.

Oh, yeah. That's how.

"What do you want my answer to be?" He nuzzled her neck as he drew back, slowly this time, his wide cockhead dragging along her sensitive, inner passage.

"I want you to say—"

He suddenly drove deep and she gasped the word, "Yessss!"

He chuckled, then picked up the pace, thrusting. In and out. Impaling her over and over. Driving her hard against the rock. His big, muscular body crushing her against it, then pulling back again.

"Storm. Tell. Me," she said, each word punctuated by a thrust.

She was so close, pleasure rising in her, swelling to incredible heights. "Will. You. Ohh . . ."

He thrust hard and deep, his breathing labored.

"Marry." Thrust. "Me?"

His jaw clenched and he ground her hard against the rock.

Then he groaned out the word, "Yes." His whole body was crushed tight against her, and she could feel him erupt inside her. "God, yes."

The joy bursting through her almost sent her to orgasm, but then he began to move again, pushing her pleasure higher and higher. She clung to his shoulders as he drove deep and hard, like a rhythmic piston.

She felt the overwhelming wave of ecstasy grip her and she moaned, then exploded into a blissful eruption of pure joy. Tears welled from her eyes as the world expanded to an infinite source of delightful, mind-melting pleasure.

As she sank back to the physical world, she leaned her head against Storm's shoulder, her legs still wrapped around him, and simply enjoyed the protective closeness of his big, strong body. Right now she was between a rock and a hard place, and life had never been so good.

"Does this mean you and I are now engaged?" She pressed her lips to his shoulder, tracing the line of one of his tattoos.

"As a matter of fact it does." He kissed the top of her head, then stepped back, still holding her close.

She straightened her legs and then he scooped her up and carried her toward the beach.

Once on shore, he settled her onto the grass. "Come on. I have something for you back at the house."

After a quick shower together, Melanie and Storm settled into the living area in his private suite, still in their robes.

"I wanted to get you a special gift and I know how much you like nail polish," he said.

She nodded with a smile.

"But," he went on, "since I gave Jessica a bottle of nail polish to express my love, I wasn't quite sure how to make this more special than that. So it occurred to me. Jessica wanted something inexpensive, that didn't use the Ranier wealth. You haven't put any such requirement on me, so I went out to buy the most unique bottle of nail polish that exists. Something that is one of a kind, just like you are."

Melanie took the small box, wrapped in black glossy paper with a white bow. She unwrapped it carefully, ensuring she didn't tear the paper.

Storm grinned. "You know, it's the gift inside that's special, not the paper."

She nodded, but proceeded with care. Inside she found an elegant black box. She opened it, and gasped.

She'd seen this bottle in many blog posts. It was one of a kind. Everything about it said diamonds. The bottle was faceted. The polish was infused with diamonds. And even the platinum cap was studded with diamonds.

"But this one bottle costs—"

"It's not polite to discuss how much it cost." His eyes glittered with amusement because neither of them much cared about politeness in that way. "Anyway, a large portion goes to charity."

A part of her felt she should reject it. It was too extravagant. Too *insanely* extravagant.

But Rafe Ranier could afford it, and if she rejected that . . . if she rejected his wonderful gesture which was based on him wanting to give her something very special, wouldn't that in a small way be rejecting him?

He smiled broadly. "Good. I can see by your face that you've decided to accept it." He pulled her into a kiss. "I wanted to give you something as unique as you are." He kissed her again, his lips brushing hers tenderly. "Now I have something else for you, too. Something to match your new nail polish."

He pulled something from his robe pocket and held up a purple velvet box and opened it. Inside was a lovely solitaire marquis-cut diamond ring.

"Oh, Storm. It's beautiful."

He pulled the ring from its cushioned bed and slipped it on her finger. She stared at it, light glittering from its faceted surface.

"I . . . don't know what to say." Tears of joy swelled in her eyes.

"Say you love me and will always be by my side."

She smiled, her heart aching with the intensity of her love for him. She cupped his face. "Storm Ranier, I love you and I will always be by your side." Then she kissed him.

He rolled her back on the couch and prowled over her. The nail polish bottle dropped from her fingers and

landed on the carpeted floor, and was immediately forgotten as Storm opened her robe, exposing her naked
body.

Life with Storm would be wild and crazy, and filled
with joy. And together they would realize all of their
dreams.

Fulfill all your wildest fantasies
with *Opal Carew*...

Read More from Opal Carew

"Beautiful erotic romance...real and powerful."
—*RT Book Reviews*

🦁 St. Martin's Griffin